You Are My Love Forever

By the same author

The Girl I Love

Myra loves Kairav and she does not even remember since when. Not just his best friend, she is also his partner in a successful dream startup.

Kairav has broken up again and turns to Myra, his best friend, for relief.

Time is running out and she needs to take control of her life before it's too late. And it's not like she does not have choices – there is Akhil, who would commit to her the moment she says yes; and Ratan, who would like to woo her to the altar.

Except that Kairav objects to her admirers, much to her annoyance.

Will Kairav ever figure out a relationship beyond his no-commitment status, to discover the girl he loves?

You Are My Love Forever

AMIT NANGIA

Srishti
PUBLISHERS & DISTRIBUTORS

Srishti Publishers & Distributors
A unit of AJR Publishing LLP
212A, Peacock Lane
Shahpur Jat, New Delhi – 110 049
editorial@srishtipublishers.com

First published by
Srishti Publishers & Distributors in 2021

10 9 8 7 6 5 4 3 2 1

Printed and bound in India

To Arpita.

You are my love forever.

Acknowledgements

Foremost, I would like to thank the characters of my book – Tarun and Neha. Their story is the heart of this book. Despite the tragedies in your past, you have found your love forever, and maybe this book will inspire others to find their true love as well.

I want to thank the love of my life Arpita for motivating me to follow my passion of writing. I have said this before, but I will say it again – I love you more than my life itself… I always have. I always will. You are my love forever.

Deepest gratitude to my family, for the endless encouragement and unconditional love.

To my brother, Anuj – thanks for always challenging me to be true to myself. To my sister-in-law, Parul – for believing in me. Thank you so much for your unwavering support. I wouldn't be doing what I love, if not for both of you.

Jayanta Kumar Bose sir – The industry experience you have and the way you can see through and find the right content always inspires me. Every time I meet you or get feedback from you, I learn something new.

A huge thanks to Arup Bose. Thank you for coming up with brilliant ideas for the book, promotion and providing so much support, encouragement and enthusiasm. Thank you for taking the time to read this book several times and providing valuable feedback.

I want to thank my editor, Stuti, for keeping me on track, answering my numerous emails patiently and with a big smile. Thank you for editing my book and for giving me the right feedback time and again.

I'm lucky to have the support of an entire team of awesome people at Srishti Publishers, a truly honest publishing house which has really brought in new talent over the years and given multiple bestsellers to the world.

Saving the best for last – my son Avi and my nephews, Vidit and Savir. Thank you for loving me unconditionally and giving me the energy to do what I love.

Readers make writers, and in this book I have tried to share a part of my heart with my valuable readers. At the end of every chapter, you will find pieces of my heartfelt honest beliefs and confessions which I have learnt the hard way – by losing someone, but then finding true love in everything I did. These few lines are the summary of the long transformation I went through. It changed my life for the better, and I hope they add something to yours.

1

Bareilly, 2009

Tarun jumps up in bed as he hears him shouting at the top of his voice. He is starting to get scared already. *What the hell happened? Did someone go against him again? Was his father drunk again?*

"You have not done anything for this family or our marriage. You're just a…"

He is shouting at Tarun's mother. Tarun is furious, but just as scared on hearing his father's fuming words. He knows that there is no meaning to such fights and it's been this way for many years now. When he was a kid, he always wondered what the real reason for the fight was. But as he grew older, he understood that the fights were mostly for no reason. It's not really a fight, as no one else has a say anyway.

His father is an alcoholic, exceedingly aggressive and cruel.

Tarun hears the sound of a glass shattering against the dining table and his hand automatically lifts up to his face, feeling the crest of the long and deep scar running along the base of his jaw. This was a gift from his father, when he threw a beer pint at Tarun. When the school principal enquired about it, his father told her that Tarun had fell off the swings in the park. And the worst part was, like everyone else, she too believed it.

In the living room, Tarun's beloved mother starts crying.

"Now don't you start crying, you stupid woman! That's not going to stop me."

His father's voice becomes thunderous, more brutal. He is petrified and tries unsuccessfully to shut the voice out by covering his ears with the pillow. He thinks he should stand up for his mother and save her from his father's wrath, but he knows from past experiences that it just makes matters worse. He knows he is just twelve years old and it's too easy for his father to beat him up. This is true for everyone in the family, old or young. Even his mother can't stand up for him if he is in the line of fire.

No one in the neighborhood believes Tarun when he asks for help. No one, except Aditi. She is his only friend who stands by him through thick and thin. They clearly share a special bond because Tarun dares to sneaks out from his window to meet her. Aditi wants Tarun to stand up against his father's torment, but he is never able to sum up the courage to do it. She keeps telling him that things can spiral out of control if something is not done about it.

Tarun knows that things have been miserable, but not completely out of control.

Not until now.

Tarun hears them fighting on the stairs near his room. His mother's light footsteps on the stairs are followed by the loud, deadly 'thump' of his father's police uniform shoes. He was discharged from the police nearly five years ago after he broke his spinal cord in an accident, but he still wears those shoes all the time. It's apparent that he is frustrated from not being accepted in the police force anymore. He has resorted to drinking even more from whatever money he has made under the table and his wife's earnings through her administration job.

Now the fight has reached just outside Tarun's door and he can hear his father's monstrous voice a few inches away. He can hear the cries of his mother as his father slaps her across the face again and again. Tarun remembers Aditi's words and wants to go and stop him. He tries to get up, but his feet don't move.

Suddenly, his best friend Aditi's innocent voice cuts through the argument. "Excuse me, uncle. Please don't hit aunty!" mumbles Aditi. Her voice is shaky with fear and sadness.

Tarun wonders what she is doing here and how she got into the house. While he is shell-shocked with her courage, he is terrified for her. He knows that his father is drunk and angry – not a good sign.

Tarun sums up all the courage and takes a few unsteady steps towards the door, only to stop. His feet betray him again.

He hears a thunderous slap and Aditi's scream. This is the first time his father has hit someone outside the family. It seems he is too drunk to know what he's doing.

Tarun tightens his fist. He wants to go out and stop his father.

He hears his mother crying and requesting his father to stop. But the more she tries, the louder the sound of slaps grows in the otherwise silent house.

Tarun runs to the door, but his hand freezes at the door knob. As he tries to unlock the door, he realizes that the door is locked from outside.

His head is spinning and his legs shake as he tries to walk through the cloudiness which grips his thoughts. He is determined to protect Aditi, but his mind is shouting at him to go under the bed and curl up into a ball. The whip of his father's belt slices into Aditi's leg and her scream of agony sends a shiver down his spine.

He is sweating profusely and his t-shirt is clinging to his body. He paces back and forth in the room as his father pushes his mother against the door. Something falls off the wall and its glass shatters on hitting the floor.

He looks at the shattered frame of their family picture clicked some years ago. They were all smiling in it.

Tarun gathers his wits and runs around to the back of the room, pushing open the window. He squeezes through the railing – which he has done many times in the past – and jumps out, goes down the drain pipe and comes running back to the front door, to face his father and protect his best friend Aditi.

Just as he opens the door of the house, he sees Aditi rolling down the stairs and his father looking at her with his belt in his hand.

Aditi falls on the floor with a loud thud and her eyes are now searching for Tarun.

Tarun looks at her in disbelief. She slowly closes her eyes, losing consciousness.

I am late. I kept thinking about saving her, but did not have the courage. I should have come earlier. She kept telling me to stand up for what is right, but I didn't!

"She deserved it. Putting her nose where it doesn't belong," his father says to Tarun. "And if you don't listen to me, I will beat you up too."

Tarun looks at his father with bloodshot eyes, unable to control his rage. He runs across the stairs and stands in front of him, facing him, looking into his eyes for the first time ever.

Tarun starts pushing and punching his father blindly, unable to control his anger.

But his father is too strong for him. He pushes Tarun with ease. His mother is screaming in shock. "You just run away, Tarun! What the hell are you doing? He is going to kill you!"

"All my life, I have been running and hiding from him, and look what he has done!" Tarun screams at the top of his voice as he gets up to his feet. "I am going to make sure he pays for his sins!" Tarun runs down the stairs.

"Where do you think you are going, Tarun? Come back here!" his father shouts in a shaky voice.

Tarun eyes his father's mobile phone lying on the dining table below and runs for it. *I have to call the police.*

He runs towards it and grabs it. The moment he presses the first digit, he feels the whip of his father's belt on his calves and the mobile falls. He kicks back his father and skids towards the mobile, picks it up and runs towards Aditi's house, dialling the police for help.

He keeps running as the number dials in and he states the whole incident in one go. He suddenly trips and falls over a rock. He spins around and falls facing the sky. Everything looks hazy. Nothing seems certain. The tears that he held tightly in his eyes start to leak and run down the side of his face. The face of his unconscious friend – and probably his first and only love – keeps flashing in front of him.

I should have stood up for her. This would have never happened if I was with her. I will never forgive myself. I hope she forgives me.

> "*The saddest summary of life contains three phrases: could have, might have, and should have.*"

2

Shimla, years later

Neha wakes up to a chilly morning and looks around, rubbing her eyes.

She loves her small rented apartment in the foothills of Shimla. She pushes off the sheet from over her and walks up to the small balcony. The cold wind howls and the morning air is freezing. Neha hugs her sweater around herself. Thick groves of cedar and oak lining the creek give her privacy from her neighbours.

She likes it here in Shimla, with its mountains rising to cut the sky and its valleys filled with towns, farms and forests. She loves the smell of clean mountain air, the taste of a sweet, cold stream, the silence of the woods, and most of all, the fact that no one knows about her past.

The smell of cedar fills her head, mixed with earthy damp. Nearby, something scuttles in the leaves. A bird chirps.

She walks into the bathroom, brushes her teeth and takes a quick bath. She wears denims and a warm hoodie. That's like her entire wardrobe. She runs her hands through her hair and ties them in a ponytail. She grabs her backpack and jacket and she's at the door calling out to Ritu, her flat-mate. "Ritu! Are you ready? We will get late for college."

As she waits there, she sees Ritu rushing out of her room doorway in black slacks, matching dress and a wafer thin body-hugging jacket. Her watch all shiny, dangling from her hand and her shoes all too clean. Her hair is done up in curls that indicate that she has spent long hours on it, and they look fabulous around her pointed little face. It looks as if she is dressed for a date. But that is who Ritu is; always dressed up.

"Hi, Neha!" Ritu waves as she approaches her, flashing a huge smile.

Ritu is a skinny little thing, gorgeous to the core. Calling her simple would have been kind. She had the most extraordinary eyes, like a twilight sky or a deep mountain lake. Her clothes were of average quality, but she had a knack of wearing them better than any other college girl.

"Hey!" Neha tries not to sigh too loudly.

"How do I look?" she asks. She quickly pops out her mobile, takes a selfie and then she pulls Neha close to her and takes another. She clicks with a pout on her face and Neha just looks blankly, rolling her eyes. She wonders why Ritu is so obsessed with selfies.

"You know you are not going to post my picture, right?"

"Yes, yes! I wouldn't post your picture on social media." She nods as she brushes her hair one last time before reaching the door. "I know you don't want the world to see you. But I am definitely going to post mine."As she swings open the door, a cold gush of air pushes almost right into her, and she turns back and shuts the door.

"What's wrong?" Neha asks, her brain processing her rigid stance, especially the hardness in her face.

"Can you not feel that wind, Neha?" she asks between clenched teeth. But before Neha can say that Ritu is hardly wearing any warm clothes, she asks, "It's freezing out there, Neha. Can't we wait inside for the bus?"

Shimla is cold, hushed, but beautiful. Even after spending nearly four years at the JUIT campus at Shimla, Ritu has not gotten used to the cold weather. Neha pushes open the door and almost drags Ritu out of the house. It's their daily ritual.

"How can we wait inside for the bus? Won't we miss it that way?" asks Neha.

Ritu rolls her eyes as her teeth chatter. Neha looks back at her. "Really? We can't have this discussion every day," she says to Ritu. "I can't figure out why you chose this campus which is on the hills? What else did you expect on the hills, duh?"

As they walk past the oak trees towards the bus stop, Ritu raises her hands in the air which have gone completely white because of the cold. "I wasn't expecting a blockage of blood circulation, though." Ritu hugs her arm, tucking her head against Neha's shoulder. "Do I really have to go to college today?"

Neha softens. Deep down in her heart, she knows she is happy for having Ritu around her. She knows she would be completely alone if Ritu wasn't there. She takes Ritu's freezing hands and rubs them between hers, trying to warm them.

Neha feels the chills too, but she doesn't want to miss the bus as the walk to the college is an uphill walk of three kilometres. JUIT has a hostel inside the campus, but that is usually given to freshers. Most seniors move out of the hostel after the first year itself and find better accommodation or private hostels. The only disadvantage is that it feels like commuting to the Mount Everest every day.

The tattered, rusted, quivering bus pulls up to the bus stop, and they race up the shaky aluminum stairs. Some other students and people push in behind them – way too many people for such a small space. Even in this cold weather, the bus is now full of perfumed and non-perfumed sweats from innumerable students and other travellers. The bus moves towards the college as Neha watches the streets of Shimla.

She loves to look at all the shops, stores, cafes and everything that is located along the Mall Road. As she looks up, it reminds her of the historic scandal that happened at the Mall Road's intersection with the Ridge road called the Scandal Point. She wished her knight in shining armour may take her away from all the darkness in her past, just like the British lady who eloped with an Indian Maharaja from the Scandal Point. Some said that the Maharaja was banished from the locality which led him to settle in his own summer capital in the beautiful hill station called Chail.

'I guess such love stories existed only in ancient times. I don't think I will have such a love story in this lifetime,' Neha sighs.

Ritu grabs the window seat and Neha sits next to her in the middle of a long seat. At the next stop, lots of people come in; like extra luggage getting packed into a small suitcase.

Two stops later, the girl sitting next to them gets up and a guy grabs it. Neha gets anxious as he sits too close to her. The world goes black. There's a loud buzzing in her ears. Her eyes refocus like an automatic camera that can't get it right.

He touches her right leg with his as he pretends to yawn and stretch. Her heartbeat accelerates. Neha hates how some guys try to take advantage of girls by almost molesting them in public places. While this is just the beginning of the act and many girls in the college have got used to such minor molestations, she isn't able to stand it. She looks outside the window past Ritu and tries to divert her mind, but she can feel herself shivering. *I can't breathe. I'm going to suffocate.*

Ritu understands her situation and knows how anxious Neha becomes in such cases. She immediately pops up from her seat and pushes her shoulder. "Where are you lost? Don't you have to get down at our stop?" She makes a failed attempt to wink at her, but she is really bad at it.

Ritu almost drags Neha out of her seat, giving a stern look to the guy. She purposely digs her heels into the guy's foot. "Oh sorry, I didn't realize I was touching you." She says to the guy as she pushes past him. The driver pulls the bus over to the stop and Neha follows Ritu to the door.

"I get these panic attacks all the time," Neha says. "It's so embarrassing."

"Are you feeling better?" Ritu asks, with a concern in her voice.

"Yes, thanks for being there, again," Neha mumbles as a small smile curves up her lips.

"You know you don't have to thank me. I know how nervous you get in crowded places," Ritu replies, in a comforting tone. "Are you sure you are fine?" She wrinkles up her nose.

Neha's smile turns up into a full-blown grin, realizing that Ritu is pretending that the crowd in the bus is the reason for her getting tensed and not the guy. Her discomfort eases down a bit. She feels lucky to have a true friend like Ritu. "Yes, I am feeling fine now."

The air outside is gusty and crisp. Ritu knots her arm around Neha and they walk the remaining distance to the college together.

"In the attempt to help me out, now you will have to walk to the college in this cold weather," Neha says, feeling guilty.

"I don't fucking care," she says. "My ass has grown fat, eating the Chinese food and the pizzas that we keep ordering. Some walking might just help shed those cheeks."

Neha begins to laugh. She finds it really funny when Ritu uses dirty language to say such a simple thing. No one looking at her would believe that she does so.

Neha is happy to have found Ritu in the first year of college when she came crying to Neha to share her personal secrets as they were too overbearing for Ritu to keep in her heart. That day Neha knew that she had found a true friend, a person who was as broken as she was. She would never hurt her.

I know her experience has been as tragic as mine, if not more. I know her parents died in a car accident. So we look out for each other. It is a given that we would be there for each other.

"The next time you see that guy in the bus, tell him, if he can't take a bath, he can at least use a perfume, okay?" Ritu grins at Neha with her eyebrows raised.

Neha bursts out laughing and the heavy feelings of guilt and fear disappear completely.

"So, how does your schedule for today look like?" Ritu asks.

Neha believes in planning everything she does. She has notes and a check-list for the whole month, all neatly planned out. She does not like unpredictability.

"Maths exam," Neha says, "that's the highlight of my schedule. I was up all night studying for it. Didn't you notice?"

"Oh yeah, I guess your room's light was on when I came back from poker night. I missed you a lot as I had Preeti as my partner. She isn't good at all. Simran and Rohit are big time cheaters, you know. They have eye signal and hand gestures to tell each other about the cards. I felt left out and alone."

Neha smiles, knowing well how this poker game would have gone. They all stay nearby and gather around at their apartment on some evenings to play poker or watch a movie. Ritu doesn't like Rohit much. He has been dating Simran forever now. In fact, some people tease them to start a family and raise kids. They are so much into each other that they definitely can guess each other's cards in a poker game, either telepathically or through some cheat codes.

The day brightens up a bit, with the sun trying its best to peek out of the overhead clouds, as they walk towards the college. They reach the most prominent building on the Mall Road– the yellow Christ Church, reputed to be the second oldest church in northern India. Ritu loves the Christ Church. Many times, she stops Neha anywhere on the road to show her the silhouette of it, from a few kilometres away, telling the tale of 1860s when Colonel Dumbleton donated this clock to Christ Church.

As they cross the clock tower, Neha looks at her watch and realizes that if they don't start walking a bit faster, they won't reach college on time.

"Wait wait wait!" Ritu says as she pulls Neha to a stop.

She pulls out her mobile, clicks a selfie with the clock tower, and posts it on Facebook. She has a weird obsession with this place and almost does it regularly, like a ritual.

"If you are done, can we move ahead? I have an exam."

"Yeah, that too on a Friday. Who the hell keeps an exam on Friday! I feel so bad for you. Actually, your teacher is a frustrated single guy, so he has nothing better to do."

"Not all single people are frustrated. Look at you! You are not frustrated."

"It's different. I am special. You know." She smiles.

"Ya, right! How many classes do you have today?" Neha asks as she gasps for breath on the steep road.

"I have just three classes, so my Friday is kind of shining." Ritu winks at Neha.

"I have an exam and you have just three classes, how is this fair?" Neha rolls her eyes.

"We should go out and celebrate later today," Ritu speaks animatedly. "Let's go to the Winsum Hills Bar and have some warm liquid to counter this cold."

Neha doesn't want to be a letdown and spoil Ritu's mood. But she just looks down and says, "Err… Ritu, you just saw what happened in the bus. You know, I can't manage being around so many people."

Ritu elbows Neha warmly as they reach the campus gate. "Don't be a spoilsport, Neha! You know you are going to crack that exam and then we can have a great party. After all, it's the weekend. You've got to give yourself a chance to do things that normal youngsters do."

"I do normal things, and enjoy spending time with you too, Ritu," Neha protests. "But when some strange guys try to come close to me, you know I can't manage that."

"You never even try to go out, Neha. I hate to think of you, always being by yourself. It's been so many years, you know. You've got to try, sweety! For me? Pretty please? "

"I definitely know how long it's been."

"Then, come out with me. We'll have a few drinks together."

Neha shakes her head continuously like an Instagram boomerang. "You just saw how I couldn't handle sitting next to one strange guy in a bus, and you want me to come to a bar where there will be many drunken guys? Like, for real?"

Ritu stops, holds Neha from her shoulders and turns her around to face her. She flashes a serious look-into-my-eyes-and-listen-to-me face. "Have you ever thought?"

"What?"

"Where will we be at this time next year?"

Neha shakes her head.

"We will be in some corporate jobs, working our asses off for a godforsaken boss, or pursuing M.Tech or MBA, or running around to make our ends meet. We will never have this time again, when we both are together, with no worries."

"Hmm."

"We may not be together next year, Neha," she says solemnly "We have been friends for three years now and I haven't ever forced you into such a thing. But I care for you and want you to open up and overcome your fears while I am around."

"But—"

"I want to know you will be fine next time a guy sits next to you in a bus. Can you assure that to me?"

"A… umm… I am not sure about that," Neha quietly looks down at her Converse canvas shoes, covered with the morning dew. "I totally understand what you are trying to do, but it's not as simple as you are making it sound. You know that. You know everything that happened. Then how can you—"

Ritu immediately comes closer and hugs her tight.

Neha hugs her back and tries to calm herself down.

"Do you understand what I am saying?" Ritu asks, letting her go.

Neha smiles back. "Yes, I do."

"Yipeee… you are coming then?" Ritu jumps in excitement "Oh! You are totally gonna have a great time, I promise you."

> "*You are blessed if you find that one special friend who brings something new in your life and inspires you to see the universe in a totally different way, who sees you through tough times, stands by you when you are left alone and loves you without judgment.*"

Neha finishes the maths test in no time. "This has to be the easiest maths test I have ever given," she whispers to herself. She rolls over the pages and checks again if she has missed out anything and cross-checks with the question paper.

She looks at her wrist watch and is surprised to realize that she has finished the test in less than half time. Her face goes red thinking about how she is going to make a scene when she submits her paper. She does not like to become the centre of attention in any situation. She likes to hide in the shadows and be invisible and non-existent in most situations.

She whiles away some time, but then gets very restless sitting in the chair doing nothing. She sums up her courage and rises up from her seat. She looks to her right and sees a guy, scratching his head to find the answers. As if they are stuck up there somewhere and if he scratches the right spot, they will fall out.

Tarun is unaware of this girl who has already finished her test while he is still stuck on the first question. He thinks his life is hell, but then he remembers he was born in hell and this is way better. He tightens his grip on the pen and tries to concentrate on the test so that he can finish it and go to the bar in the evening with his flat-mate Gaurav. Usually, he is the last one to agree to go to a pub, but tonight, his friend has somehow convinced him to meet at the Winsum Hills Bar. Where else could he take him? There were very few decent bars in Shimla.

Straining to focus, he shifts back on his seat and massages his temple as if it can silence the last night's nightmare that was still screaming in his ear.

"Damn it!" he groans, rubbing his eyes and trying to shake himself out of it.

The shadow of someone on his answer sheet pulls him out of his reverie and he stares up to see Neha, who is nearly standing up from her chair. He checks his watch and looks up, and then again looks at the watch. And then, back at her! He is surprised.

"Really? Please tell me that this isn't true. You couldn't have finished the exam!" Tarun says with a tone of shock in his voice. Suddenly, everyone in the class turns around to look at her.

Neha turns around, dumbstruck and confused as to what to say to this guy. She gets really nervous as everyone is looking at her.

Tarun wonders why she isn't responding and is looking so pale and worried. Maybe, she doesn't know the answers to the questions and is going to flunk anyway. Maybe, he made her too conscious of this fact, so he quickly speaks back to her to settle things in the right way.

"Hey, don't worry, it is just an exam," he tries to relax her. "Even I don't know the answers to most of the questions. In fact, I was waiting for at least one student to submit the answer sheet so that I could get saved from the embarrassment. Thanks!" He shows her a thumbs up with a wide grin.

He thinks his comment would cheer her up, but it makes her more upset. Somehow, he just can't stop looking at her. She looks so beautiful in the sunlight streaming through the windows – her long, beautiful nose, her slender arms, her hair in neat, pretty waves, but stuck under the hood of her jacket. It's as if she is purposely trying to hide her beauty.

Hazel. Her eyes are hazel.

As her brow furrows, her eyes brighten. They look like the cover of a mystery novel, holding a lot of secrets inside them. They are full of despair and fear, which reminds Tarun of someone, but he doesn't want to spiral to those memories. He knows what happens when he goes down the rabbit hole of his childhood memories.

Neha wonders how to react to his comment. She has actually answered every question and is sure to get good marks. “Actually… I… It’s not like that.” She’s breathing too fast and her eyes aren’t focusing. It’s as if she’s having a panic attack. She looks at Tarun and notices the long faint scar near his jaw.

Tarun is surprised by the anxious look on her face. She looks sad, angry, tender and lonely. *It’s just an exam, girl. Failing in an exam isn’t the worst thing that can happen to you. There’s a lot worse that can happen. I know because it has happened to me. I lost my one and only love when I was a kid and now I can never meet her again.* Tarun wants to say these things aloud to her, but he just keeps looking at her.

Why do guys stare? They are all the same and they remind me of Dheeraj. And that is someone I don’t want to remember, Neha thinks. *I can’t be here anymore. I need to go. I am not sure if he is like him, but I am sure that I need to go away from here. From him. From everyone.* Neha immediately tenses up, reliving the memory, unable to keep it locked out.

The professor watches the commotion and shouts out loud. “What’s happening there?” he says, looking at Tarun. “Are you trying to cheat from her?” he looks sternly at Tarun.

Tarun mumbles to himself. “How can I cheat from her! She herself doesn’t know any answers.” Then he quickly looks back into his paper and pretends to write something very seriously.

The professor looks at Neha. “What happened? Why are you standing? Do you need something?”

She widens her eyes at his rapid-fire questions. With trembling hands, she walks up to the professor and hands him the completed answer sheet.

Now the professor’s eyes widen. He extends his hand to take the sheet.

"Have you finished the paper?" He's surprised. "Really, Neha?"

Neha nods. She feels that the whole class is piercing her back with their gaze. She can barely breathe; something is strangling her from inside. Automatically, her feet race down the corridor and up the stairs, looking for a place to just be. She pushes through the doors of the library and it's somehow lighter here. There are only a few kids scattered throughout the entire library. No one even looks up at her.

The librarian – a woman with black-rimmed glasses, steps forward with a stack of books in her arms. She smiles at Neha warmly. "Hello. Are you looking for something?" she asks, setting the books down on the counter.

I am looking for a place to hide, I want to tell her. Just hide me from the world. And never make me go back out through those doors again. But she doesn't say anything. She just can't.

> "*Have you ever wanted to crawl into a hole and disappear forever? Well, I have. When I lost someone close, everyone kept asking me – How are you feeling? Is everything OK? And I wanted to shout at their face. No! Everything is not OK! It will never be OK. And I want you to leave me alone.*
>
> *But somewhere deep down, I wanted to live again. And I could do that by changing just one letter in my life.*
>
> *'How I will live my life' to 'Now I will live my life'.*"

3

The college corridors are flooded with students, trying to get out and enjoy their Friday. Neha is on her way home. Ritu is walking alongside her, talking enough for the both of them. Neha tries to stay close to the wall as they walk. She hugs her books to her chest to make herself smaller, to be her armour.

Neha isn't listening to what Ritu is saying; she is lost in her own thoughts of how she caved in today because of a small incident.

How will I live my life? Any small situation that puts me into the focus of others, makes me want to crawl back into a shell. Just because of the incidents in the past, I am not able to live in the present. I just don't know how to handle this. All I do is think about one thing only. The thing that keeps me up most nights.

Tarun is swaying his notebook as he wanders down the Mall Road. He makes his way through a group of tourists, pawing through bins of souvenirs at a hawker and wonders about how many refrigerator magnets would people buy? In fact, most of them were made in China, so they were not really a souvenir from Shimla.

"Oye, Tarun! I am here," Gaurav raises his hand and waves from the other side of the street. He's sitting on a wooden bench opposite the well-known Krishna bakers. This is their favourite spot for time pass while returning from the campus.

His mouth is stuffed with a mutton momo (dimsum) and he has a veg *kurkej* plate waiting on the bench for him. He pulls down his hoodie and brushes the hair away from his eyes.

"Hi Gaurav. How much are you going to hog?"

Gaurav quickly gulps down another momo from the plate and tries to hide away the plate of veg kurkej from Tarun, without looking at him.

Tarun just gives him a look. "Dude, it's not as if a famine is going to strike. You don't have to eat so much."

He waits for a response. Nothing. Gaurav chomps away to glory.

"Dude, say something!"

Gaurav wrinkles his nose and then, his right eyebrow goes up. Looking at Gaurav, Tarun starts to feel a bit hungry himself. As he tries to pick a kurkej, Gaurav pulls away the plate, imitating Tarun, "Dude, it's not as if a famine is going to strike. You don't have to eat so much," and pushes him away from the food.

Tarun loses his balance and collides with a short girl walking by. She loses her balance, stumbles forward, and is almost about to take both of them crashing on the floor. But Tarun somehow steadies himself and averts the fall with great difficulty.

"What the fuck! Are you blind or what? Can't you watch where you are going?" She pushes Tarun back as she steadies herself on her feet.

"Oh, I am so sorry. Actually my friend pushed me—" He turns around to point at Gaurav but sees him sitting with his back towards them. *What an ass!*

"I'm sorry. I didn't mean to hurt you," Tarun repeats his genuine apology.

Suddenly, her expression changes from anger to a warm smile as she looks over his shoulders. "It's okay," she says, steps past Tarun and walks up to Gaurav. Her smile broadens as her eyes lock with Gaurav's.

"Hey Ritu, what's up?" They high-five and then give a low five-clap as if it's their ritual.

"So, you are meeting me tonight, right?"

"Yes definitely. Winsum right?"

"Yes, where else?"

They talk a little but Tarun isn't able to hear them. Before he can say something, Ritu starts to leave. "I need to leave; my friend is waiting for me. I'll see you in the evening." She waves back at him.

As Tarun turns around to see who her friend is, he sees a girl standing away from this commotion, holding her books tightly to her chest. That is Neha, the girl with the hazel eyes.

She smiles up at Ritu, an adorable, godlike smile, and holds out her long arms. Ritu walks up to her and they say something to each other and start laughing.

Tarun wonders if this is the same terrified and nervous girl he saw in the morning. All her hesitation and breathlessness is gone! She is smiling, blushing. Both of them! They walk further, smiling, arms around one another, and Tarun can't help staring at Neha.

Her hair is the color of coffee beans, swaying as she walks. She looks like one of those naturally beautiful girls who have no idea how pretty they are. She dresses casually and has a gorgeous smile.

As he is lost in her beauty, Ritu turns around and looks angrily at him. Her possessive and protective message is loud and clear. It feels as if she is saying – 'Don't even think about it!'

She says something in Neha's ears and their laughter heightens. Neha turns around to see the guy that Ritu has told her about, and her laughter vanishes upon spotting Tarun. Her eyes are locked with Tarun's and her mouth forms a perfect circle of surprise.

The surprise is soon replaced with fear and Tarun is unable to understand why he is causing this reaction in her. *Is she worried that I would tell others that she knew nothing in the maths exam? Why is there so much fear in her eyes?*

Tarun tries to lock away the gates of a painful memory, but it's too late. The fear in Neha's eyes opens the flood gates and the memory is live in front of him.

The memory he wants to forget. The memory he *can't* forget.

In less than a second, his eyes are closed and he feels dizzy. His heartbeat accelerates. He shakes his head and tries to take a steady breath. It doesn't work. He holds the nearby wooden bench, but his hands tremble.

That look in Neha's eyes brings back his worst nightmare, as if it were happening right now!

He can see Aditi's eyes. He sees the fear in her eyes.

"Are you alright?" asks Gaurav, holding Tarun.

"I am fine," Tarun blatantly lies, to avoid confrontation. But in his thoughts, his childhood love Aditi is rolling down the stairs of his house. Again. She hits the ground with a loud, horrible thud and Tarun vigorously shakes his head as if it will help in making the memory disappear.

He pushes Gaurav aside. "I need to go, I'll see you later," Tarun snaps and stomps down the road.

Neha is still dressed in her jeans and hoodie when Ritu walks in from the bathroom, spritzing herself with a delicious vanilla fragrance.

Neha is startled when she notices Ritu standing in front of the mirror. She looks like a goddess in her white dress that accentuates her hourglass figure. It looks perfect against her fair skin. Her hair is wavy, cascading down her back. She looks like she's ready to go to a beach party in Goa.

She asks as she fastens her hoops through her ears. "How do I look, babe? Stunning?"

"We're not going to a beach party." Neha smiles. "It's just a bar full of people. But touch wood. Mmmuaah, you are actually looking stunning."

"I know." Ritu gives her a smile as she smoothes down her dress.

"Aren't you going to get dressed up?"

"Don't you think you are pushing your luck?"

"Okay, cool! I will back off. I am glad that at least you are coming with me."

They both smile and Ritu gives Neha some air kisses next to both her cheeks as she doesn't want to spoil her makeup.

They head towards the Winsum Hotel, but the mob inside the top-floor bar causes Neha to pause. She looks at Ritu, who in turn holds her hand, assuring her that everything will be fine.

The bar is packed tonight. The tables have been removed and an army of college students, all dressed up, are drinking away to glory. The waiters are maneuvering trays of beers through the swarm of bodies. Some waiters are even holding five mugs with their five fingers, flaunting their serving skills.

As they make way through the bar, they are greeted by Gaurav. He turns to them and bows his head like a gentleman. "Shall we?"

"Yes, of course," Ritu responds with a matching twinkle. She looks at Neha and simply nods and follows them.

They walk up to the bar and grab the few bar stools available. The clamour of excited voices and the peculiar Bollywood music makes the room unusually loud for Shimla. "It's like New Year's Eve in here," Ritu shouts.

Gaurav bends down to shout back. "But not the real one. This is more like that glamorous, fake one you see in films. I always spend the real one watching television alone in my bedroom under a blanket."

"Exactly! I think more than half the citizens of our country do that," Ritu responds animatedly.

"Thank you Shimla for allowing alcohol to be legal."

"Thank god we have this bar, else we wouldn't have any place to go out," shouts Ritu, but Neha cannot disagree more. Her hazel eyes are expanding to the size of saucers as she scans the bar. The noise is piercing. People are walking like they are riding a merry go round, cursing and laughing at the stupidest things. Guys are shamelessly hanging onto girls, trying to get their attention. The smell of the bar is a mixture of smoke, sweat and booze.

Neha whispers to Ritu, "This is where you have been begging me to come? Like, for real?"

"Yeah, it's not bad once you get used to it."

Ritu leans in to Gaurav and asks, "So your friend, what was his name…"

"Tarun," Gaurav adds.

"He hasn't come with you? I thought he was planning to join us."

"I wonder where he is, baby!" he replies. "He behaved strangely after you two left and then disappeared."

Neha gives him a death glare for using the word 'baby', but Ritu seems to be okay with it.

"Isn't that weird?" asks Ritu.

"No, not really! He hardly socializes with others. He usually likes to spend time alone."

Ritu eyes Neha and whispers in her ear. "Doesn't that sound like you?" She giggles and Neha elbows her to shut her mouth up.

Meanwhile, Gaurav starts talking to the bartender. He turns around and asks, "So what's your poison, ladies? Ritu, will you still have your favourite drink?"

She nods with a big smile plastered on her face. "And Neha will have a Cosmo cocktail."

Before Neha can disagree, Gaurav turns around and explains the order to the bartender.

As Gaurav is busy ordering drinks, Neha whispers to Ritu, "Who is this guy and how does he know your favourite drink? And why is he calling you baby? Am I missing something?"

Ritu smiles at her comment and whispers back, "I used to date him in the first year when I was too lonely. But he was too good for me. I didn't want him to feel stuck with a broken girl like me."

Neha remembers Ritu telling her how she had dated a lot of guys to fill the void in her life. It actually helped in making Ritu more confident and happy.

Just the opposite of what Neha would have done.

"So, here we are! Cosmo for Neha, Cherry mojito for Ritu and Bacardi with cranberry juice for me."

"Really, you still drink this cough syrup? Grow up, dude!" Ritu rolls her eyes and sips her drink.

"You are the one with fruits in your drinks, and you are questioning my taste buds. Really?" snaps Gaurav in a taunting tone.

"You will never change *na*?" Ritu asks.

"Why would I change something that's perfect *na*?" He imitates her tone.

She punches his shoulder and laughs.

Their conversation lingers on and Neha wonders if they were actually separated after the first year.

"Is Tarun the same guy who collided with Ritu today?" Neha asks when she sees a pause in their conversation when they sip their drinks.

"You mean the guy who wanted to snatch my beloved momos?" Gaurav grins. Neha simply nods. "Yeah! That's my friend and roommate, Tarun."

Ritu stretches a megawatt smile across her face. She has never seen Neha inquisitive about a guy.

"Do you think he's handsome? Are you interested?" Ritu asks Neha while setting her drink on the table.

"Umm... No," Neha stammers as her brain goes blank. "I think I have seen him somewhere, that's why I wanted to know. Nothing more." She looks down at her drink to avoid eye contact.

Why is Ritu cornering me in front of her friend? Doesn't she know I am never interested in any guy Neha wonders.

"Tarun is single, in case you are interested," Gaurav grins. "But he is a tough nut to crack."

Neha's eyes widen to triple size and she shakes her head left to right to deny his request.

"Actually I haven't seen Tarun with any other girl. He is a gem of a guy, a bit strong on the outside, a little weird on the inside. But I think you both may get along."

"Just stop it, Gaurav!" Ritu turns around in her seat and glares at him.

"Hey, I am just trying to help—" Gaurav continues.

"That's enough!" Ritu raises her voice.

Gaurav finally takes the cue and Ritu changes the topic. Neha takes a small sip of the Cosmo and tries to relax herself a bit. She watches them talking, reminiscing their past. *If only I could reminisce my past. If only I had even one good memory to look back to.*

"Hey Neha, are you alright?" asks Gaurav.

"Ya, I… I'm okay. It's just that I usually don't go out too much, so…" she says.

Ritu jumps in to save her from this awkward moment. "Neha doesn't like being at crowded spaces."

Gaurav is unable to understand what this means, but decides to let it go.

Once the focus of the discussion shifts from Neha, she feels relaxed. The alcohol in the Cosmo has started to kick in and she wonders if she is liking or disliking it, because it's making her enjoy the moment. She is feeling less guarded and free, which worries her too.

Gaurav suddenly tells Neha, "I have been thinking who you remind me of."

Neha raises her eyebrows and asks. "Who?"

"Tarun! Yes, you are exactly like him."

"Not again," intervenes Ritu.

"Why do you say that?" blurts Neha inquisitively.

"He behaves just like you, Neha," he replies. "I have to literally beg him to go out with me. He likes to stay in isolation, and even though I was able to convince him to come tonight, he suddenly had some panic attack and decided otherwise."

"Are you serious?" Both Ritu and Neha ask in unison.

Gaurav gets intrigued by their sudden interest. "Yes, I don't know what's wrong with him, but all he does in his life are two opposite things!"

"What do you mean?" asks Ritu.

"Standing up for a girl. And, staying away from girls."

"What are you saying?" Ritu and Neha looked puzzled.

"Confusing, right?" he raises his eyebrows. "Let me explain. A few days back, Harsh was ragging a fresher and she started crying. Tarun happened to see this. He came running and literally stood between Harsh and the girl. He asked Harsh to back off and leave the girl alone."

"Then?"

"Then what! You know Harsh; he is a real bully. He continued to trouble the girl," Gaurav stopped to take a sip of his drink.

"Then, what? Don't pull us into a story and stop in the middle," Ritu snapped.

"The next minute, I see that Tarun has punched Harsh square in the face and he is now lying on the floor." Ritu's eyes widen. "So now you get it? It's crazy, right?"

"Why do you say it's crazy?" Neha says. "It's so nice of him to stand up for her."

"True! The weird part is that the girl fell for Tarun. She wanted to go out on a date with him."

"So, did he go?" asks Ritu.

"No, he didn't! He did the opposite. He started avoiding her or hiding or disappearing whenever she came his way."

"OK. That is definitely weird," says Ritu.

But that is not how Neha feels. She is intrigued by Tarun's actions. She wants to meet him. Even more. She wonders if this erratic behaviour is because Tarun is as broken as she is. Maybe, she could trust him. Maybe, he would understand her better than others, because he had a tough past.

Suddenly, Neha hears a loud thud which shakes her out of her thoughts. Gaurav has just gulped down his drink and banged the glass on the table. Ritu is glaring at him as if she will pluck his eyes out.

"I think we need to call it a night," Ritu gets up to go back home.

"Wait, wait!" Gaurav says.

"What?" Ritu replies.

"Many many happy returns of the day," says Gaurav in a slurry and tipsy voice.

"Are you drunk already, Gaurav? It's not my birthday," Ritu says.

Gaurav grins. And the grin is really wide and reveals a rarely seen pair of dimples.

"No really, happy birthday, Ritu," he says as he writes something on the back of a Heineken paper coaster and folds it and gives it to her. "As you didn't tell me your birthday, I have made one up myself."

"Really, a coaster for my birthday?" she asks. "And what have you written on it? If that's your phone number, I am going to kill you."

He gets down from the bar stool and folds his hands. He says *namaste* to Neha like an air hostess would. "It was nice to meet you, and I hope next time we can chat more. Right now, I need to go because Ritu can murder me anytime."

Neha smiles at his cuteness. She bids him goodbye and turns to see Ritu, tearing the coaster into two.

"Don't tell me! Did he really give you his number?"

Ritu steals her eyes away from Neha and looks elsewhere. "Yes," she says.

Neha feels that there is something fishy. "Show me what he wrote… please, Ritu."

"No!"

"Don't worry, I am not going to steal his number and call him," Neha says jokingly.

Before Ritu can realize, Neha snatches the two halves from her. Her eyes widen as she reads the note:

Tarun Sharma
8826262626
Introduce him
to Neha.
They're made for
each other.

"You are right. I don't need this." Neha's face turns red and she hands the torn halves to Ritu. "I actually met him in my math exam today. It was pretty weird."

"When were you planning to tell me that?" Ritu says excitedly.

"There is hardly anything to tell," Neha says

Ritu's piercing stare makes Neha squirm. "Ritu, don't push me for this. I have nothing to tell right now."

"I am not going to push you into anything. That's why I tore this stupid coaster in the first place." Ritu shoves the coaster into her purse and orders another drink.

Now that Ritu is off her back, Neha takes a deep breath and gulps down the remainder of her drink. *I could have told Ritu how I felt about Tarun, how his deep eyes intrigued me, how I am still thinking about him, how I want to meet him again. But I know she will jump to conclusions and think I am interested in him.*

> "*Grief comes into our lives uninvited. It is difficult to know how to steer our feelings in the course of such massive change like losing someone you love or some other tragedy. It can often feel like you're the only person experiencing what you're feeling, but the silver lining is that you are not alone in the experience. Whatever stage of the grieving process you're in, there are people all around you who've been through hard times too and can help you feel less alone. You just need to allow them to be there for you.*"

4

Tarun lay on the couch, restless as hell. He is staring blankly at the ceiling and his nightmare is playing on loop in his mind.

Aditi is lying unconscious with the impact of rolling down the stairs. I wish I had listened to her and decided to stand up against my father. I have betrayed her trust. I can never forgive myself for not being there for her when she needed me the most. However hard I try for redemption, it just doesn't help. I have tried to channelize my pent up anger on assholes in the college who bother innocent girls, but the guilt of not being there for Aditi just doesn't go anywhere.

Gloomy and horrified eyes clutter up his thoughts and he is no longer able to distinguish if those eyes are of Aditi or Neha. He can see the same fear in them.

He is unable to understand why Neha is scared of him and the way she looked at his scar. He places his thumb over the scar. That opens up Pandora's Box of dark memories he has kept locked inside his mind.

He is ten again, crouching on the floor of the living room, his father standing in front of him with bloodshot eyes.

He crouches further as his father hurls down the pint of beer from the dining table on to him. It shatters on his jaw, cutting him across the length of it and he howls in pain. He tries to pull away the piece of glass stuck to his jaw, and the moment he does it, he winces in pain. He can feel the stream of blood gushing out.

"I wish you were never born, Tarun! I am fed up of your stupidities."

Just like many other times, Tarun is unaware of the reason of his father's anger – alcohol, failure in his police job, a failed marriage or something else. He wants to fight back, but he doesn't; his mother has begged him not to.

He hears his mother's scream from somewhere behind his father. She envelopes him with her arms, trying to act as a shield against his drunk father as he continues to hit him with whatever comes in his hands.

He hears the sound of another glass shatter near him, but he doesn't open his eyes. He knows that if he sees his mother in pain, he is going to kill his father.

He remembers his mother taking him to the family doctor, who fixes him as nicely as he can. At least, the stitches and medication would heal his external injuries. But what would wipe away his internal scars?

The loud sound of his mobile jolts him. He looks around in perspiration and picks up the phone as a message vibrates in his inbox. It's Gaurav.

You're coming to SISC next weekend with us.

Tarun is unable to understand what's going on. He is unable to differentiate between his dream and reality. He looks around to check if his father is still around, but soon realizes that he is no longer in that house. He is safely lying on the couch in his rented apartment in Shimla. He takes a deep breath and sips water from the bottle lying on the floor next to the couch, before messaging Gaurav.

SISC? Why the hell are you talking in code language?

He cannot help but think. *Am I not confused already with so many things in my life?*

Gaurav: *Dude, which world are you living in? You have been here for three years! Remember the Shimla Ice Skating Club? The one next to Lakkad Bazaar.*

Tarun: *And why do you think I would go ice skating? I don't know how to skate. Last time you took me there, I almost broke my back, trying to stay on my feet.*

Gaurav: *We all will have fun! I promise.*

Tarun: *Who 'we all'?*

Gaurav: *Why do you want so many details, dude? Just trust me and see for yourself.*

Neha is fighting her demons in her nightmares. She can hear her heart pounding. She is terrified. She knows this nightmare too well.

She remembers being fourteen again!

She is sitting on the sofa in her elder brother Manish's apartment and reading a book. She sees her elder brother walk into the living room with his bag.

"Where are you headed? I thought we were going to spend time together?"

"I know you have come to spend your holidays with me, but I still have a few classes left. My break starts in four days. I guess mom got confused with the dates."

"Oh! I wasn't aware of that."

Manish understands the frustration in her voice and puts his bag on the couch, sitting next to her.

"I don't want your holidays to go waste. I understand that mom and dad are super busy in their office and they sent you here to meet me. But I have some classes to attend in college. I will try and finish early and come back by 5. Does that work for you?"

She nods. He hugs her lovingly and then walks to the main door. "I have stocked up the refrigerator with your favourite stuff. So, you can have whatever you want."

She smiles at his sweet comment and waves him goodbye.

She lies down on the sofa with a book. She reads for some time, until she hears the sound of the lock on the main door clicking. She looks up elated, expecting to see her brother.

But her smile turns into a frown when she spots Dheeraj, her brother's roommate. He is taken aback to see someone inside the house, but his surprise doesn't stay for too long.

"Who is this beautiful little girl on my couch?" he asks with a sneer in his voice.

"I... I am Manish's sister... here for my holidays," she manages to squeak, trying to look away from his leering stare.

She has somehow always disliked him. Now that he keeps staring at her, she hates him further. She feels scared by his gaze. Like he is looking at her as a piece of flesh and not as his friend's sister.

"Oh! But where is Manish and why has he left you alone?" he momentarily shifts his eyes from her to the clock on the wall. "When will he be back?" he asks.

"He had some classes. I think he will be back by 4," she replies, suddenly feeling too cold and scared to realise that her brother isn't going to be back for long.

"It's okay, I am here," he replies and walks close to her and sits next to her on the couch.

A loud knock on the door wakes Neha up and she sits upright, panting in fear. She is twenty-one, in Shimla, in the apartment she shares with Ritu. Dheeraj has disappeared. Her night dress is sticking to her, soaked in sweat. Her heart is literally thumping out of her chest as she looks around her room, coming to her senses.

She looks at the small round alarm clock on the bedside – 11:30 a.m. She hears the loud banging on the door again.

"Open the door, Neha! It's afternoon already," Ritu shouts from the veranda and Neha jumps up to reach out for the door.

When she opens the door, Ritu comes barging in. "Are you alright? We need to talk! You can't keep sleeping all through the weekend. You had promised to spend some time with me and then…"

"I think I am too over-worked due to the classes and assignments." Neha is ready with her excuse even before Ritu can complete her rant.

"Don't you dare lie to me!"

Neha realizes that until she tells Ritu what's going on, she won't let her go. "Ritu, it's just that I don't feel like going anywhere."

"Just follow me! You need to give some answers." Ritu stomps out of the room.

She heads for the refrigerator and pulls out the box of chocolates as Neha tiptoes behind her. She has this strange but delicious tradition of having something scrumptious when there is some distasteful or uncomfortable talk to be done. She believes that it nullifies the effect.

"Sit!" Ritu points to the couch.

Neha quietly sits on the couch. She eyes the dark chocolate. The happy hormones that kick in with chocolate are not new to her. In fact, the best is chocolate-dipped strawberries.

Ritu jumps onto the sunny patch of the sofa and keeps the chocolate box between her and Neha. Neha picks up one and eases immediately.

"So here is the question – We stay in the same apartment, but did we meet yesterday?"

Neha thinks of the best way to answer this tricky question. "I was in my room all day…"

"Please answer the question! Did we meet?"

"Er… No."

"And why would you do that?" Ritu snaps back at her.

Neha doesn't like being scolded. She avoids answering by looking down at the box of chocolates. She can feel Ritu's eyes, piercing daggers into her.

Ritu calms down, "Listen, Neha! I care about you." She picks up another chocolate and puts the box on the table, moving closer to Neha. "I am really worried."

"Just let it go, Ritu! I didn't ask you to take care of me," Neha snaps back.

"Don't tell me what to do! I have all the right to be worried about you. Do you get it?" Ritu replies.

Neha is taken aback by Ritu's reaction. There are undertones of fear in her voice. She has never sounded like this before.

"Neha, you are my only family and I don't want to lose you, like I lost my parents."

"Ritu, I didn't mean to upset you. I am sorry, it's just that…"

Neha doesn't know how to tell Ritu about the nightmares – how they are getting from bad to worse, or how she is thinking about Tarun after meeting him just once. She has never let any guy come close to her, forget letting him into her thoughts.

Ritu continues to stare at Neha and then hits her with a chocolate. She misses and Neha laughs at her failed attempt. She pulls out the cushion from behind her and hurls it at Ritu. Ritu ducks and the pillow goes flying behind her, making both of them laugh.

When the laughter fades, Ritu says, "Neha, you need to face your fears and start meeting people. You can't keep yourself locked down in your room. How do you think you are going to manage when you start working? Or, when you move to some other college for your Master's degree?

"I know, but—"

"Shh, just listen! You need to trust me."

"I do trust you—"

"If that's the case, I am going to tell you something and you are not going to kill me for that? Is that okay?"

"Why would that be fine? Maybe you have done something worthy of making me kill you," Neha laughs back.

"I told Gaurav that we'll go to the ice-skating rink next weekend."

"Why would you tell a guy that I would go out with him?"

"No! I told my friend that *we both* will go out and spend a good weekend," she justifies her response.

"With or without you, I am not going out with a guy."

Ritu loses it completely. "What happened with Dheeraj was ages ago. Every guy isn't Dheeraj! You need to move on and heal if you—"

"Easy for you to say. He didn't rape you." Neha hisses, practically spitting poison and shaking in fury and fear.

"I didn't mean it like that," mumbles Ritu.

"You were not called a slut, you were not assaulted and you haven't lived with nightmares every night!" Neha continues shouting.

"Neha, I am sorry…"

"Who do you think you are? That you can be there for me, change things because there is no one for you? Not even your parents!"

Her accusation strikes with an unexpected force. The last bit reverberates around the room. Neha realizes that she has crossed the line. She wants to wipe away the words but the pain they have caused is visible in Ritu's eyes.

Ritu lost her parents in a car accident and grew up without the love from her family. She was raised by her mother's sister and hasn't gone back to her house since she joined college. This *is* her home. With Neha.

Neha is fighting back tears as she turns to Ritu. "I… I'm sorry, Ritu. I don't know what I was thinking."

Ritu continues to stare outside the window without any expression on her face.

Neha offers her a chocolate but there is some sadness which a chocolate cannot counter.

"I will go ice skating with you. I will do anything to bring back that smile on your face." Neha tries to cheer Ritu up, tears trickling down her own face.

> *If you are living in the past, it is difficult to find meaning in the present. Acknowledge that it was the past and it is over, and it cannot harm you any longer.*
>
> *Work hard to trust someone in your present and take the first step with him/her, so you can be free!*

5

The next few days are unsettling. It seems that both Neha and Tarun are aware of each other's presence and it affects them.

Whenever they see each other in the classroom, a chaotic energy surrounds them. It rattles the air between them. It buzzes and hums. And every time, their eyes meet, a shock wave jolts through their system.

The professor paces the front of the classroom, lecturing with wild gestures about the mathematical equations while Tarun is busy figuring out the equation in his life.

Tarun is intrigued and wants to know about Neha more. Neha is sitting a few seats away to his right. He looks towards her but turns back to his books. He doesn't want her to get nervous again. But the moment, he turns his eyes away, he feels as if she is looking at him.

After much control, he finally spins around to see Neha but quickly turn back to his notepad. A small smile curves up his lips. He tries to focus on his book, but his mind keeps wandering back to her.

When he looks at her, her long brown hair is lightly whipping against her face. *God , she is so beautiful and perfect, every inch of her.* It looks like she is purposely trying not to stand out in the crowd by toning down her dressing style.

"That brings us to the end of this topic," the voice of the professor reverberates in the silent room. He looks around and picks up a stack of papers. "Now I will distribute the results of your math exam."

That brings Tarun back to his senses. "Oh god, I am going to fail." He stiffens up and then smiles. *Maybe this is where I get to talk to Neha. I think when both of us fail in the exam we will have something in common and we can bitch about how difficult the exam was.*

There is a flurry of discussions around the classroom as the students start talking to each other.

The professor calls out names and Tarun sees most students walking back with a sullen face. He looks at Neha but she is sitting expressionless. As if, the result doesn't matter, or she knows the result already. He wonders how she is calm when she is going to fail.

The professor finally calls out Tarun's name and he walks to take the sheets hesitantly. 41/100. He spins around in joy! "Yesss!" he says as if he has topped the class.

The professor gives him a look and there is an awkward silence in the class, followed by roaring laughter.

Neha is still looking down, scribbling something in her notepad.

"I would like to announce the result of one student specifically," the professor announces. "Neha, please stand up!"

'*I knew it.*' thinks Tarun. She left the paper in one hour so she must have got the lowest marks in class.

"99/100! That's her score!" the professor stands up and claps for Neha, all other students following his lead.

Tarun is completely flabbergasted. The girl who left the classroom in half-time with tears in her eyes scored 99%! That too, in such a tough, god-forsaken exam.

For the first time in my life, I am feeling shocked, speechless and dumb – all at the same time! That day when she left the classroom, crying, it wasn't because of the exam. It was because of me! But what have I done? Why such a reaction? ponders Tarun.

The dismissal bell rings and he sees Neha moving towards the exit. He doesn't want a girl in his life, but he can't stop himself from getting attracted to her. He feels a strange magnetic pull towards her.

"Neha?" Tarun blurts out. The moment the word escapes his lips, he wonders why he did that!

After an uncomfortable pause, she raises her head in surprise and glances uneasily at him. She points a finger at her chest. "Me? Are you calling out to me?" she asks hesitantly.

"Congratulations!" he says, not having anything else to talk about.

Her expression falls back into that familiar blankness. She shifts uncomfortably and hefts her slipping bag back over her shoulder. Her face is unreadable.

"Umm, thank you," she says after a long pause and disappears outside the door. Neha is thinking about her rendezvous with Tarun. The discussion was pointless, but she feels much different than the last time. She usually spends time in the library, but today, she decides to head home.

Neha walks the next few steps in silence until she crosses the corridor to the main exit gate of the campus. She listens to the faint crunch of gravel below her feet. The air is cold and she feels the chill on her nose as she walks towards her apartment.

Why did he call out to me? Did he want to talk to me? Probably he wasn't sure what to say, but just wanted to have a conversation with me? There's nothing wrong with that! Then why did I walk away? What do I do with all the marks in my exams when I am incapable of making conversations! I just don't know how to be a normal person again.

She tries to lock the thoughts away. She isn't able to make head or tail of what's going on. She walks quickly down the steep stairs to her apartment. She can't feel her fingers as she tries to use the key to unlock the door. She holds the lock, yanks the key inside and throws open the door.

Ritu smiles at her but gets no response. Neha quickly closes the door behind her and runs across the room.

"Yay! I am so happy you are back. I just—"

"Later, please!" Even before Ritu can finish, she interrupts her and walks to her room. "I need some time. Alone."

"Listen, Neha—"

She enters her room and loves how warm it is. Ritu has already turned on the heater for her. *Oh god! How sweet can she be! And look at me, being so rude to her! But I just don't know how to manage my trapped feelings. I need to vent out my feelings and I don't want to lose my temper on her.*

She picks up her diary to write, her way of venting out all that is going on in her heart so that she can clear her mind. Her tattered Harry Potter bookmark takes her to the empty page and she sits down on her desk and begins to write.

Hey Diary!

My eyes kept wandering off to Tarun during the Math class. I just couldn't stop myself from looking at him. Once or twice, when he suddenly looked back, I quickly ducked and started looking elsewhere. The weird part is that while I wanted to look at him, the moment he looked at me, I couldn't look into his eyes.

I am unable to understand why I like looking at him. And why am I scared of him? Do I like him? Or do I find him to be really cute?

Even worse, when he tried to talk to me, I gave him a curt, one-word answer! That's what I do. I shut the doors to my mind so that people cannot continue having a conversation with me. I felt humiliated that I couldn't sum up the courage to talk to him and my words disappeared into the pit of my stomach.

Thankfully, I didn't start crying or he would have felt that I am a weirdo.

Why do I care if he feels that I am a weirdo? It has never mattered to me what others think about me.

Surprisingly, though Tarun started the conversation, even he was speechless. It was as if I was seeing a mirror image of myself.

I am unable to talk to him. And he is unable to talk to me. But probably, I have started liking him. That makes it even harder for me to talk to him.

Do I really like him?

Neha sighs in exasperation and stares at the page, her heartbeat pounding in her ears. She draws three crooked stars under her diary entry, places the Harry Potter bookmark back before closing the diary. *Maybe it's enough for now! Or maybe not?*

She immediately opens the diary, holds the book mark and flips the pages right to it.

She strikes out the stars and continues to write.

The problem is that I think I am starting to like Tarun, but he may finally end up like Dheeraj. I too want to go out and have a normal life. I feel frustrated when Ritu begs me to go out on weekends, but even if I really try to convince myself, I am so scared, that I finally give up.

She draws three solid stars under the line, puts back the bookmark and closes the diary firmly. She takes a deep breath and feels a momentary sense of calm. But the calmness is short-lived.

"Oh god, I am in a deep mess!" She curls her hand around her thumb and squeezes it.

She looks at the diary and flips it around before opening it. She wants to write more, something she does not want to remember. She usually writes stuff she does not want to read again at the end of the diary. She hopes that one day the good things in the front will outweigh the bad things in the back, thereby liberating free from her past. It hasn't happened yet, but she believes in it.

I am fourteen and sitting on the dining table chair. My mother is cutting vegetables to prepare dinner while watching her favourite program. My father is in office and

I am trying to sum up the courage to tell her about what happened.

She is too busy watching television. I am afraid she will get really angry with me and maybe throw me out of the house.

I need to tell her that Manish's roommate raped me!

He threatened me that he would make sure to find me and hit me till I die if I ever reveal the dark secret to anyone. He even threatened to hurt Manish if I did so. While I have tried my best not to tell anyone, it's eating me up from inside. I am starting to get scared of small things which used to be so normal earlier. I hate going to any family gatherings, weddings or even the playground.

I start sobbing at minor issues. I get angry or run away from people and keep myself locked in my room. This isn't me. I need to repair myself. I can't live like this. I need to tell them what really happened so that Dheeraj pays for his sins, not me!

It's taken me forever, and my father is back home. It is tougher but I cannot endure hell alone.

Just when I am about to call my father out, he turns around and looks at me.

"Did you see that?"

"What?" I am confused.

He points to a girl on the television screen. "You see, this girl, she is spoiling the name of her family. She used to go out with all sorts of guys and now she has come back home, crying. Does she think her family will accept her? After she has behaved so irresponsibly? A girl needs to behave herself and stay away from such people. After all, it'll be her loss in the end."

I stare at the television, unable to make out what's going on. My eyes fill up with tears. Maybe he is right. It's the girl who loses in the end. Maybe it's always the fault of the girl. She is the one who got herself raped. That is how the society sees it.

"I am happy that our children and the kids around you have been raised well," he says, proudly.

"But what if this happened to one of these kids you know and trust?"

"You must be out of your mind!" he says snobbishly. "All the kids I know have been raised well. No girl would get herself raped, I know!" He flips to the next news channel and turns his face towards the television.

I feel worse than before, realizing that my own father has such a regressive mindset. Get herself raped? Is that even possible? Who am I living with? Who are these people? With an increasing heartache, I get up from the chair, feeling hopeless by the fact that I cannot even truly express my feelings to my own father.

"You wanted to ask something, Neha?" he asks as I head to my room.

I turn around and simply say, "No, nothing Papa !" I don't even feel like calling him papa anymore.

I can tell that he really wants to talk to me, but I am not sure if he will understand.

As I try to speak, my breath hitches in my throat.

"Are you okay? You are looking really pale?"

I stare at him nervously, his eyes stab into mine. "Yes," I manage to say.

"If you need to talk about something, you know I am there for you."

"Y...yes." I say quietly at his hypocritical and ironic comment.

I am being executed for a crime that I haven't done. I am being executed without anyone listening to my explanation. I am being executed because I couldn't stop myself from getting raped!

Neha finally closes the diary. The venting-out-ritual is over. "I wish you die a painful death, Dheeraj, and rot in hell."

She looks at the clock and feels bad at making Ritu wait for her. "She is a godsend angel. What would I do without her?" Neha says looking up at the ceiling.

Neha walks in to the living room and sees Ritu sitting with Preeti and Simran. Simran is a sweet girl who stays in the neighboring apartment, but isn't a close friend of Neha. She actually thinks that Neha is a nut case and something is seriously wrong with her.

"Oh, I forgot to tell you," she says to Ritu on seeing Neha, "I had to call Rohit, so I'll see you later." She quickly makes her way to the main door.

Preeti follows suit. "Hey Simran, wait for me! I need to go to the market."

As the door shuts, Ritu turns to face Neha. "How are you feeling now?"

Neha smiles, knowing just how lucky she is to have Ritu.

"I feel much better, thanks for understanding," Neha answers as she helps Ritu clear out the table.

"Do you want to discuss anything?" she says, picking up the empty cola glasses from the centre table. "You know I am a good listener," Ritu winks.

"I just wanted to apologize to you," says Neha. "I am sorry I was rude to you and said bad things about your parents."

"Where is this coming from?" says Ritu. "I mean, discuss why you were upset today?"

"I really mean it, Ritu. I shouldn't—"

"You really mean what you said?" Ritu fakes shock.

"Oh no. I mean, I didn't mean what I said. I mean I am sorry for the things that I wasn't meant to say."

"Can you listen to yourself?" Ritu laughs out and hugs Neha firmly.

"You forgive me?"

"No, I haven't forgiven you."

Neha jerks back and looks into Ritu's eyes.

"I can forgive you on one condition." Ritu adds. "You are going ice skating with us and that's final!"

"Okay, if I have to!" Neha shrugs.

"Cheer up, girl! It's not like I am asking you to jump off a cliff."

"That would have been easier."

"Trust me, this weekend is going to be a life-changing moment for you!"

Neha looks at her excited eyes. *I wish it changes everything. I have tried in the past too. It's a truly awful thing to live in terror and I wouldn't wish it for anyone.*

> *"There are times when you cannot discuss certain things with your parents. Create your own family and surround yourself with real friends who are willing to accept you with all of your pain and insecurities. Who will stand by you at your lowest points."*

6

"My god! What are you wearing? Your woollen cap clashes with your gloves," Ritu says to Neha. "And, they look even worse with that jacket. Would you, like, die or something if you dressed up a little better, Neha?"

Neha pulls down the black woolen cap further over her ears. She links her arm through Ritu's and marches her out before she can say anything else. She doesn't like getting dressed up at all. That too, for a day at the skating rink which will be full of strangers.

They start their walk towards Lakkad Bazaar. She loves to come here for a walk as the market has a history of its own. She looks at the wooden toys placed in the shops made by a small group of Sikh carpenters who settled here a century ago. While, some may not realize this, but Shimla is so multicultural and yet aloof from where she is. That's why she likes it here.

Neha continues walking through the small lanes, knowing well Ritu could make her stop anytime. Ritu loves Sita Ram for its famous *aloo tikki* and *chole bhature*. Surprisingly, today, Ritu chooses to walk past the market, across the DAV School, straight to the skating rink. Neha wonders why Ritu is so excited for ice skating.

Neha enjoys the mild sunlight, streaming in through the clouds. It's a perfect day for ice skating. The thickly forested hillside that offers shade to the Shimla skating rink gives it an unparalleled ambience.

They finally arrive at the skating rink and stand in the queue to issue the skates of their respective sizes. Once they have their skates, Neha sits on a bench nearby and takes a deep breath. She hasn't gone ice skating for long and relaxes herself so that she can ease into it again.

Neha bends over to wear her skates. As Ritu comes and sits beside her, Neha breaks into a loud laughter.

"What happened?" asks a puzzled Ritu.

"You can't be serious. Purple skates! That's what took you so long."

"What's wrong with that?"

"Is this for real, Ritu? Purple skates with purple cap and gloves? And you were judging my dressing sense!"

"'Ha ha." She cooks up fake laughter. "Very funny! And what about your woollen cap covering your eyes? I am sure it will help you find your way on the skating rink."

Neha tugs her cap further down and Ritu starts laughing. They're laughing together now, not even sure why.

They enter the skating rink gracefully, holding hands like performing artists, but just as they start to feel good about it, Neha loses her balance and falls flat on the ice, pulling Ritu down with her. They stumble down laughing.

"Oh, my jacket is completely wet," Neha says, but she's still laughing.

Ritu starts laughing so hard, she clutches her stomach.

They're laughing, completely blissed out.

Ritu gets to her feet easily, then offers her hand to help Neha. Neha takes her hand and stands, holding it for a second to regain her balance.

"It's good that we fell before Gaurav came. Else, it would be too funny and embarrassing."

"Ya, true that! But where the hell is he?" Ritu looks around the skating rink.

"Hiiii Gauuuuuravvvv!" Ritu shouts at the top of her voice. "There he is, let's go!" She looks at Neha and starts skating towards Gaurav. "I think he has company."

Neha could barely see Gaurav, leave aside the company. She tried to focus but all she could see was a decently-built guy wearing a cap, jacket and scarf. His friend seems to be a clumsy skater as he keeps falling. On any other day, Neha would have objected to the presence of another stranger with her, but today was different. Today she was feeling happy. *Maybe I can be like normal people and enjoy simple things in life.*

"I want to show you my favourite spot." Gaurav stretches his arm towards her and Ritu grabs his hand. They speed skate further away with their hands clasped together.

"Hey, where are you going?" Neha calls out behind them, but they are already gone.

Neha is skating after a long time, so she turns around slowly and skates to the corner of the rink. She skates along the circumference in silence and the hush feels peaceful. She feels good, free and after a very long time, she is able to enjoy simple pleasures of life.

"Sometimes I should appreciate the fact that I live in Shimla. I feel like I am floating in an ocean," Neha feels oddly pleased to say this aloud.

She starts skating with tentative strokes and then slowly builds up the speed. She isn't sure why she is feeling so happy today. Was it because the day started well, or because the rink had only a few people, or was it the perfect temperature? She didn't really care. She swayed freely across the ring like a dancer, performing to her heart's content.

She is gliding, having forgotten that she came with Ritu, Gaurav and his friend. She takes a deep breath, enjoying the spicy aroma of the cedar trees. She feels a subtle difference in the smells between winter and summer.

"Thankfully, everything is going fine today," she says to herself.

The moment she utters the words, a skater crosses her at a great speed and she suddenly loses her balance. *Oh, no!* She closes her eyes as she falls, the cold sting of the ice smashing to her neck. She hears the *swish-swish* of another skater coming closer.

"Are you okay?" A guy stops right next to her. The moment he looks at Neha, his eyes go wide with shock.

So that's why Gaurav forced me to come skating today! He and his ex-girlfriend have set all this up. I am going to break all his teeth.

Neha looks up at this tall guy with a familiar voice, standing next to her and her eyes go wider than Tarun's.

So, this is the friend Gaurav has come with! He couldn't come here with any other friend? Or maybe, Ritu set me up. I am sure she set me up. She is going to die today. Let me just get my hands on her! Neha's mind is in overdrive.

"You?" Tarun looks puzzled.

"You?" Neha looks just as puzzled. The look in his eyes tells her that he was unaware of the set up.

"Want me to help you?" he asks softly.

Neha bites her lip. "No. No. I can manage myself."

Neha rolls to her side, trying to avoid twisting her ankle in the process.

This is definitely Ritu's idea. She has disappeared with her friend, leaving me behind with Tarun, so that I try and talk to him. Huh! I am not going to do that.

"Come on! Let me help you." The only thing that comes naturally to him is to help a damsel in distress. So he offers his hand to Neha.

But Neha is stubborn. She shrugs away his hand. "Oh, I am perfectly capable of getting up."

After three more unsuccessful attempts to get up, Neha looks up at Tarun and tries to convince herself to take help from him.

Tarun looks around, his eyes searching for Gaurav. "That fucker Gaurav set me up. I am going to kill him." He almost says it out loud.

Neha smiles. *So he doesn't want to be here either. We both don't want this. That's a good start. Maybe Ritu is doing the right thing. I need to face life. At least he is trying.*

Reluctantly, she takes Tarun's hand and lets him pull her up to her feet.

Neha gets up and keeps holding his hand for a second as she regains her balance.

Tarun studies her, trying to look beyond the serious look on her face. "Neha, I didn't know about this, believe me."

She wants to tell him that she believes him, but the words just don't come out. She manages a nod.

"I want to say something more."

"W…What?"

"I am sorry for making you nervous during the exam. I really am. That wasn't my intent."

She tries to speak up, but the words get stuck in her throat. *Why the hell can't I talk to him?*

"Are you alright, Neha?" he asks.

"I am really sorry," Neha manages to say. "I am like…a sort of an introvert… and don't do good around people. I just can't manage it." Neha finally replies.

"I didn't mean to make you nervous again. I mean, I just wanted to clear things out, that's all. I will leave you at peace."

Neha tries to calm herself down. She knows it's not Tarun's fault. She is the problem.

"No, don't go!" she blurts out.

"Are you sure?" he asks hesitantly.

"Yes, you don't have to go," she says, "I am sorry for behaving like this."

His lips curve into a wide smile. "Do you come skating often?"

"Not really! But I am still decently good at it. If it weren't for that stupid guy, I wouldn't have fallen." She blushes.

"Don't worry about it. Now I am here."

Neha simply looks down on the ice and smiles. *Maybe I can trust him.* She smiles and turns to Tarun, thinking. *I can have a simple conversation. I need to try. So where do I start?*

"Have I mentioned I am not good at conversations?" she finally asks.

"A couple of times, yeah."

Neha laughs. "Okay, so let's begin from the start. My name is Neha. What's yours?"

"Neha, huh? Nice! My name is Tarun." He plays along.

"Where are you from?" Neha asks.

She sees Tarun sigh, sees him look away. *So, not a favourite subject, obviously.*

"Uttar Pradesh," he finally answers.

"Where in Uttar Pradesh? That's a huge state." Neha feels great that she has come so far. She is actually talking to a guy!

"Oh, from Bareilly," he says uneasily.

"Tired of the heat, huh?"

"Tired of the heat, the crime, yeah."

"Do you travel back much? I mean, is your family still there?"

Tarun gives a half-smile. "Full of questions today, Neha?"

"Just making conversation, that's all."

"Enough about me. What about you?" Tarun tries to avoid answering about his family.

"Umm, I can tell you, but you have to promise not to judge me."

"Oh! I will, if it deserves that!" He smiles with a wide grin on his face and Neha breaks out laughing.

"Karnal, Haryana."

"Ooooh!"

"Come on! It's a nice place," Neha replies.

"Really? Karnal? Haryana? I hear people fire bullets in the air during marriages."

Neha's laughter echoes in the valley. "Really, of all the things, you are judging my hometown for this?"

"No! I am also judging it by its narrow lanes, honking bikes, people getting into feuds over small land matters, and the entire town shutting down at ten."

"Hmm... Maybe you're right." Neha gives up. When she has no ammunition left to defend her hometown, she gets back to Bareilly.

"So you mean to say Bareilly is really hot and happening! Wide streets and night life? If you like it there so much, then why did you leave it? Huh?"

Like a shadow crossing the sun, Tarun's expression changes from friendly to distant. He looks away from her and his ears turn red hot despite the cold weather.

"I hardly go back to Bareilly," he manages to reply. "I like Shimla better."

Neha observes the rage and resentment in his voice. She does not want him to be uncomfortable so she tries to change the topic. "You are right. Shimla is so much better. That's why we are here, isnt it?"

"Yes," he says, his voice low, his teeth clenched.

Neha feels helpless. She is usually the one who drifts off in conversations. So she doesn't know how to pull him back.

"By the way, which engineering stream are you studying?"

"I have computer science as my elective and you already know I am really good at maths!"

"Ha ha, oops!" Neha smiles.

"What about you?"

"Well. Mine is similar to yours. IT engineering. So maybe that's why we have so many common subjects.

"So, what are your plans after completing engineering?"

"I am not sure. I am thinking of working with some small and medium businesses here in Shimla and help their businesses get online. It's a win-win for both – they get to sell their products online and I get to stay in Shimla. I just love it here."

"I also love this place," Tarun says, unable to hide the smile that springs to his face. "But I usually don't believe in planning the future."

"Why do you say so?"

"I want to be in control of my present. I don't want to think about the past or the future. It is not really in our control."

"You are so right!" Neha says thoughtfully. "If only I could stay in the present. Like in this moment, everything seems so nice."

"Tell me, Neha! Are you a math genius, or do you ace all subjects? I am sure anyone would love to have you working in their company, no matter big or small. Have you started applying?"

"I gave some interviews," she says, with unsteadiness in her voice, "but like I told you, I get really nervous while talking to people, so I failed every interview. I couldn't answer a single question, though I knew all the answers."

"I didn't realize that," he says. *That's so sad. The most brilliant student of the college can't crack an interview because she's nervous to face people. I wish I could help her. I wish I could hug her right now, and tell her that everything will be okay.*

"Let's skate a bit. Are you ready?" she says, trying to avoid further questions.

"Sure. You are ready to skate and I am ready to fall. I have been doing that since morning," he confesses honestly, and she can't help but laugh.

"I am telling you, it's not that difficult! Let me teach you some tricks," she chirps.

She swerves right, spreads out her arms and takes a stance. "Spread out your arms for balance; go ahead, try it."

Tarun is in awe with her beauty and simplicity. He tries to steer his eyes away from her. "But Gaurav asked me to stand straight when I begin skating," he says, wondering if he has been doing it all wrong since the last one hour.

"I think Gaurav just wanted to have some fun at your expense." She grins at him. "When you start to skate, you need to bend forward a bit and move forward by pressing your right foot forward," Neha speaks like a teacher and laughs as she hears her own confident voice.

Tarun is lost in her eyes. He tries his best to concentrate and copy her skating stance.

"God bless me and my spine," he folds his hands, looks up at the sky and prays.

Neha takes the stance and slowly moves forward, but suddenly turns back to look at Tarun.

She realizes that the stance she has told him is for a right-footed person, and not left. She forgot to check the same from Tarun. But it's too late.

Tarun tries moving ahead on his right foot, but he is unsteady. He spreads his arms wide like a joker walking on a tight rope in a circus. He keeps swinging his arms up and down and finally manages to balance on his skates. He looks at her and gives her a million dollar smile.

As Neha comes back to give him some support, a skater comes at a very fast speed and bumps into Tarun. Before he can gain some sense of balance, he falls right on top of Neha. She feels the sting of cold ice on her back and simultaneously Tarun falls over her, holding himself right above her.

As she looks at the dark figure on top of her, her mind snaps from the present into the horrible past, imagining Dheeraj on top of her. She feels scared and starts pushing her legs out and screaming out for help like a maniac.

"Get off me! Get off me!" she shouts, her eyes misting with tears.

"Listen! What happened?" Tarun is shocked, but Neha isn't listening anymore. She has blocked him out. She isn't on the ice skating rink anymore. She is on the couch of her brother's apartment where Dheeraj is forcing himself upon her.

All Tarun sees is tear-filled eyes crying for help. The pain in her eyes reminds him of Aditi and he is lost, rage steaming in his body with his own nightmare.

I should have stopped him. I shouldn't have listened to mom and kept quiet for so long. Long enough to lose you. If only I could go back and undo the past. If only…

> "*Be patient with yourself.*
>
> *When recovering from a tragedy, you might be flooded with emotions in a second and be numb in the next. This is perfectly normal. Your mind is trying to come to terms with the magnitude of what's happening, so be patient with yourself. Healing is a gradual process. Take one breath, one day, one step forward at a time.*"

7

"Neha, don't worry! I am here." Ritu comes skating to the spot where Neha is lying and tries to shake her out of her nightmare. "Look at me!" Ritu literally shouts into Neha's ears. "You are here, in Shimla, with your best friend. No one will harm you."

Neha lifts her head slowly, afraid to open her eyes. Tarun suddenly shakes his head and opens his eyes to realize what's happening around him. He takes Gaurav's hand and tries to stand up slowly, not looking at anyone as he gets up.

He sees Neha cry out loudly as Ritu helps her to the seating outside the skating rink. Seeing Neha cry, sadness grows inside him. He didn't mean to cause her so much pain. But right now, the only thing he can do is to wait patiently till the storm inside Neha subsides.

Neha looks at Ritu, her tears falling. She sobs now, leaning against Ritu and wrapping her arm around her, praying the pain goes away.

"Tarun's falling on you triggered your memories, Neha. Don't worry! I am here. You will be fine," Ritu tries to calm her down.

"I told you, I didn't want to come here!" Neha sobs, trying to catch her breath." I told you I can't do all this! I've been suffering immensely for so many years and this is only adding to the pain in my heart. I just cannot do this."

"You can't lose hope like this, Neha. I am right here with you. I know you can put all this behind. You know that too, but you need to try."

Ritu glares at Tarun, who is waiting patiently behind her. He shrugs helplessly. He is sure the girls want some space so they decide to skate away to the other side of the rink.

Once they are few feet away, Gaurav speaks up. "Is Neha mad or what? Is she like getting fits?"

"Don't you fucking say a word against her!" snaps Tarun.

Gaurav looks at Tarun as if he has lost his mind. "Did you also lose it when you fell on her? I was feeling sorry that I got you to meet her. This girl is completely insane."

"I said not a word against her!" Tarun is brimming with anger.

"You have hardly met her for an hour, dude, and you are taking her side?" Gaurav says.

"Sometimes, even a moment is enough to connect with someone," Tarun replies.

"I guess I will leave you with your philosophies. Ritu was right – you are just like her." He speedily skates away from Tarun.

Tarun tries to catch up, but falls, crashing down in no time. Ritu starts laughing and swerves towards him, helping him up. A few seconds later, Neha comes around too.

"What happened to Gaurav?" Ritu asks.

"Probably he didn't have the time to wait for an amateur like me."

Neha sums up the courage to look at Tarun and meets his eyes. She isn't sure if Tarun will shout at her for acting like a maniac or just walk away . To her surprise, Tarun doesn't deter a bit. He smiles up at Neha. An adorable, godlike smile.

"Good to see you again," he says as if nothing happened.

"So, can we start your skating lessons again?" Neha says hesitantly.

"Sure, if you are ready to put up with my falls. Because I am very good at falling." Tarun's smile widens.

She extends her hand to him. He raises his brows and looks at her enquiringly.

She smiles and nods back. "I won't bite. I promise." Neha doesn't know what's happening to her. Her heart is overflowing with joy. *As I look into his eyes, I feel a flutter in my stomach. The corners of my lips curl upwards and it almost hurts, but in a very special way. It hurts like it's the first time I've truly smiled in my whole life.*

Tarun smiles back. "Are you really okay?"

Neha nods, even though she is not sure if she is okay – or if she will ever be. "Apologies for what happened."

He holds her hand, for balance, but sees her quiver. She tightens her grip for an instant and then eases it.

"If it's okay with you, can you tell me what happened back then?"

Neha shakes her head.

"I understand," he says. He knows he really understands.

Ritu skates ahead in search of Gaurav while Neha and Tarun start skating slowly.

"That's nice! You are doing good, keep going," Neha says with a smile that takes his breath away.

"What can I say, I am good at getting passing marks!" Tarun says promptly.

Neha laughs out loud, remembering the maths exam incident.

After sharing some more tips with Tarun and seeing him catching up, Neha leaves his hand. She flips her feathery brown hair over one shoulder and skates a bit ahead, out of habit, and Tarun follows her, trying to match her speed.

He watches Neha skate, following her slowly around the oval when another skater moves past him at great speed. He tries to steady himself, but falls flat on the ice. He notices that this skater had previously made Neha fall. This guy was clearly showing off his skill by skating close to others, not considering the fact that it might hurt them.

Tarun stands up with an added energy in his veins. He watches the skater move ahead, laughing, moving very close to Neha.

"I am here, Neha. He won't hurt you this time." He didn't know how, but the feeling was strong and dangerous. Seeing the skater go closer to Neha makes it worse.

Tarun tries to catch up with him. He skates as fast as he can, so fast that he isn't sure if he can even stop himself.

The rowdy skater is cutting left and right pretty close to Neha, as if he's attempting to frighten her. Neha slows down, trying to avoid him, but he comes back and rotates around her, mocking her.

"Why don't we skate together, baby?" His voice is dripped with sleaze as he looks at Neha.

"Please don't bother me!" Neha's frightened voice soars up to Tarun with the wind and his heart pounds.

He feels anger bubbling up inside him. He forgets that he is in the skating rink, surrounded by people. He can only see the bully harassing Neha. He speeds up without any fear of falling or breaking his own bones.

He speeds past Neha as quick as a cat and before the bully can realize what's happening, he collides right into him, shoving him as hard as he could, sending him toppling down over the ice a few feet away.

"Are you out of your mind? Trying to get me killed or what?" snaps Tarun, getting up to his feet with firm determination.

The bully is completely taken aback. "What do you mean?"

"Why would you stand up in the middle of the skating rink? Don't you know amateurs like me don't even know how to stop themselves?"

Tarun remembers his father throwing blame on others with ease, making them think it was their fault. Now, he went with the flow. "I know I need more skating lessons, man! But you need to make sure you don't come in the way of the learners."

The bully got up to his feet as a cluster of people zoomed to the accident scene, their skates sounding like buzzing drones. Taking advantage of the fact, Tarun looks back and winks at Neha. She takes the cue and heads towards the exit, smiling at his sweet gesture.

Tarun is happy because he could bring a smile back on Neha's face. Because never in his life was he going to repeat the mistake he once did.

As Neha is sitting in her cosy room, she can't help but think about Tarun.

Tarun stood up for me, like no one ever has. He hardly knows me, but was there when I needed support. He is not like other guys, and definitely not like Dheeraj. But why did he stand up for me? Why did he skate so fast when he knew it could lead to a big accident and hurt him? I need to ask him.

Neha tiptoes to Ritu's room and starts searching for something. Ritu is lying motionless, as if in deep sleep. Neha looks at Ritu's table using the flashlight of her mobile. Tissue papers, assignments, cookie wrappers... where is that Heineken coaster which Gaurav gave to Ritu?

"Are you looking for this?" says Ritu and Neha jumps up in surprise.

Neha turns around and Ritu switches on the bedside lamp. Neha can feel herself blushing as she sees Ritu sitting awake and upright in her bed, with her purple mink blanket pooling around her waist. Ritu opens her bed side drawer and pulls out the torn coaster with Tarun's phone number. She holds it between her thumb and index finger, as if enticing Neha to come and get it.

"Actually..." Neha stammers.

"It's okay. Just say you want it and I will give this to you," Ritu says notoriously.

"Yes, I want to..."

Before she can complete her sentence, Ritu jumps up from the bed and hugs her tightly. She lightly kisses her on the cheek. "Muaah! Here you go. It's all yours. Oh I am sooo happy," she squeals as she dances around Neha. "I am happy that you are at least trying to talk to a guy."

"Umm... I'm not sure I want to call him. It's just that, I mean... maybe I do," she stammers weakly. "Maybe I am confused."

"You don't need to be confused. I think your confusion can disappear only if you talk to him."

Ritu gets into her cozy blanket as Neha rushes back to her room, locks the door behind her and quickly grabs her mobile. Neha sits down heavily at the edge of the bed, dialing Tarun.

Just as the phone call is about to go through, Neha feels her cheek sting, and then she is numb and so cold. She quickly disconnects the call.

"Oh god! Why am I feeling so nervous?" her knees are shaking and she tries to hold herself together. "It's just a phone call. I need to do this," she mutters under her breath.

Before dialing again, she tries to get over the instinctive and sharp pang of fear, but is unable to. "No, I just cannot do this."

She turns back and lies down on the bed. *I need to try, maybe in some other way.*

She stares down at the coaster, and her spirit lifts up at an idea. "I can probably message him. That's possible. At least that ways I don't have to face him right away."

Hi, it's me… Neha. I need to talk to you. Maybe we can grab a coffee in the campus if you are free?

She sends the message and quickly switches off her mobile. She has had a good day and she does not want to read his response tonight, because she will end up thinking about it all night.

Something is happening between us. Is it friendship? It doesn't feel like friendship. Perhaps I'm projecting my own desires and I'm confused.

Maybe, there is light at the end of the tunnel.

> "*There is light at the end of the tunnel. The tunnel represents a part of our life-journey, filled with the darkness of inner struggle. To find the light at the end, we must advance through the darkness with complete faith and hope.*"

8

"For the hundredth time, I am not going on a *date!* I am just meeting him."

"Ya, right! I believe you," Ritu gives her a dismissive huff. "You are meeting Tarun for dinner at Café Sol, which is one of the best Italian cafés in Shimla, and it is just the two of you. So yeah, damn right, it's not a date."

"I wanted to meet him for coffee in the college cafeteria, you know that!" Neha replies.

"And, how did it magically turn into pasta then?"

Neha's response is a deep, flaming blush.

Ritu lets out a cough that turns into a snort of laughter as she walks and sits next to Neha on the couch. "How did you get pulled into an Italian dinner instead of coffee?"

"You think I know?" Neha widens her eyes. "It just happened! I asked him to meet over coffee and he suggested Café Sol instead. I don't know how I agreed."

Ritu turns to Neha with a comforting smile. "Okay, I get it. It happens. So what are you planning to wear?"

Neha looks at her jeans and hoodie, narrowing her eyes at Ritu. "What's wrong with this?"

"Don't tell me you are planning to go like that for your first date?"

"It's not a date! And yes, I will go like this. Try stopping me!" Neha fumed.

"Don't be silly. At least, wear a nice skirt, sweety."

"I'll change into a new shirt. That's the best I can do."

"Why won't you wear a skirt, you have such sexy legs!"

"I haven't worn a skirt since I was thirteen," Neha snaps, unpleasant memories entering her mind.

A sickening recollection of Dheeraj moving his hands on her legs jumps out of her brain and she closes her eyes, hoping for it to go away.

"I am sorry," says Ritu. "Wear what you feel like wearing, it doesn't matter."

Neha nods numbly. "I'll take a bath and get ready."

"Neha..." Ritu calls out, seeing Neha walk towards the bathroom. "I feel proud that you are trying to make an effort. Just relax and have a good time!"

Neha stands close to the front door of Café Sol, a mere twenty minutes away from her apartment. But somehow, she cannot sum up the strength to go inside. In her effort, she walks past the entrance a couple of times.

The butterflies jostling in her stomach are a clear indication that she is looking forward to this dinner with more anticipation than she's ever experienced.

Tarun is sitting inside, waiting for her. He spots her outside the door, but is surprised to see her walking past the door over and over. He requests the manager and rushes out, using the back door. He is back at the front door and walks right in front of Neha, pretending he has just reached.

"Hey Neha! I am so happy you could make it."

Neha's throat tightens and her breathing becomes shallow when she realizes that she is actually standing in front of Tarun once again. *What in hell am I doing here?*

"I got a little late." Neha smiles sheepishly at his excitement.

They finally walk in together. The waiter motions them through a spacious dining area. A painting of the clock tower of Shimla hung above one wall and another painting of the snow-covered mountains adorned the wall to their left.

"I have a reservation in the name of Tarun," he says.

The waiter smiles and guides them to a table by the window, overlooking the valley.

Tarun pulls out the chair for Neha and helps her sit down. This small gesture brings out a big smile on her face.

The waiter places two small bowls in front of them, and then puts in a small circular tablet in each. He pours hot water on the tablet and the tablet begins to grow vertically.

Neha stares at it as the waiter smiles and says, "Please ma'am," and goes away.

"What the hell is this?" She looks and Tarun.

"I am not sure," he says. He lifts up the tab and tries opening it up, only to realize that it is some fancy wet tissue to clean up their hands.

He spreads out the tissue and drapes it over his head. Neha starts laughing simultaneously.

"Are you ready with your order?" the waiter appears unexpectedly as Tarun is busy playing with the tissue. Neha bursts out into a fresh fit of laughter as she sees Tarun straightening up and removing the tissue.

They order garlic bread, penne Arabiatta pasta and a pizza. The waiter notes down the order and walks back.

Till here, it was easy. Chatting with each other was the tougher bit.

She is scared to death. He is nervous too, but tries to start a conversation.

"Do you like the place?"

"Yes, it's fabulous," Neha says as she surveys her surroundings. "This place seems very popular. I am surprised how you even got a reservation here."

"Well, I could come back with a witty reply and say that I simply mentioned my name and a table miraculously became available. But in reality, they had just received a cancellation when I called," Tarun replied honestly.

Neha was beginning to enjoy Tarun's sense of humour and his honesty. "I like the witty reply more than the real one, let's go with that."

"There is something more I want to say."

"And that is?"

"You are looking gorgeous."

Neha's heart skips a beat at the unexpected compliment. She slowly lifts her gaze and looks into Tarun's eyes. "Thank you."

"If you don't mind, I want to ask you something," he says nervously.

"Umm, okay."

"I didn't see you in college today. What happened?"

Neha is taken aback by the sincerity of the question. No one ever asked her whereabouts, no one ever cared if she existed. Till now. "I chickened out," she says, sincerely.

"Out of what?" he asks

"I purposely didn't come to college as I thought that if I see you in college, I will get too nervous and cancel the dinner plan."

Tarun was taken aback. At that very moment, his mobile rings and breaks the tension. He hastily scans it before swiping and cancelling the call.

"I am sorry," he says. "It's my mother."

"Don't you have to talk to her?"

"Well, I will do that later," he says.

"Are you sure?"

"Sure," he says. "I need to talk to you right now."

"So how was your first experience at ice skating?"

Tarun laughs out loud. "I think you can call it my first experience at ice-falling. I could hardly skate," he says.

"Oh come on!" Neha disagrees. "Once you understood the tricks, you did well."

"Well, I was taught by the skating expert Gaurav, who had clear plans to get me killed."

Neha bursts out laughing.

"Thank god, I met you. No, seriously! Once you taught me how to do it, I really started enjoying it," he blurts. "Every bone of my body is aching, but it was completely worth the effort! You are awesome."

"Tarun, you don't know me—"

"I want to know you, Neha." *I wish I could heal your broken heart. I don't know why but I need to.*

Neha is speechless at his remark. It has been a long time since anyone wanted to know her, really know her.

Few minutes later, the waiter returns with a huge assortment of delicious dishes and places them one by one neatly on the table. Tarun serves the garlic bread and the pasta for her and then for himself.

"Listen, Tarun?" Neha gulps in some air. "I wanted to thank you for protecting me from that bully in the skating rink, and I need to know why you did it? You don't even know how to skate and you went at such great speed at him. You could have hurt yourself."

Tarun chokes on the food, sliding down his throat with the sudden question. Neha gets up and crosses the space between them in an instant, her concern plainly visible on her face. "Are you alright?"

Tarun manages to catch his breath without embarrassing himself any further. "Yes, guess the pizza decided to go down the wrong pipe. I'm fine, really. He blinks several times to clear his head. "So, you were asking me something?"

Neha returns to her chair, never taking her eyes off Tarun. "I want to know why you helped me at the rink?"

"Actually I wasn't really helping you. I was just trying to help myself.

"Please don't talk in riddles."

"Neha, I hate bullies, and have a lot of really bad experiences with one, in my past. At a turning point in my life, I decided to stand up against any bully." *I hope she doesn't ask the turning point.*

Neha smiles in return, surprised by what he said. Just listening to his honest answers is making her feel good.

"Please don't think that you owe this day to me. I did it because I hate when someone gets bullied. And God forbid, if it happens again, I'll be there, standing up against it."

"Thank you," Neha replies softly. Her voice has a huskiness that had not been there a moment ago. The promise of 'being there for her' that she sees in his deep eyes makes her throat grow dry.

I wish Aditi was here, thanking me. If only I had made it in time to rescue her. His mobile starts buzzing once more and spoils the moment. He looks at the screen and mutters something, inaudible under his breath.

"I need to take this call. I am really sorry," he says apologetically as he gets up and walks towards the entrance.

Neha can see him walking to and fro in the lobby. She can make out that he is talking to his mother. The initial few sentences are inaudible, but then she hears him scream. "I don't have to tell her!"

What his mother says is not audible to her, but he can hear it loud and clear. "What are you going to do? Just walk with her until you can't anymore?" his mother shouts.

"It's not like that!" Tarun yells.

Neha has a dipping feeling in her abdomen. She realizes she shouldn't be eavesdropping on their chat, but she can't stop herself.

"You're going to end up hurting her. Is that what you want?" his mother warns him.

"It's my life. Please just let me live it!" Tarun screams, realizing quickly that he is too loud for a public place and he lowers his voice. Neha is unable to hear the rest of the conversation.

He returns to the table, his eyes as cold as the Shimla winter, but Neha doesn't let it affect her. He's struggling with whatever it is his mother thinks he should tell Neha. She wants to know what it is so badly, but she decides to not push him.

At that very moment, the phone buzzes again and he angrily presses the power button and switches it off.

"It's okay. Whatever it is, it will be fine. Just relax!" she says calmly.

"It will never be fine," he says, through the lump in his throat.

"Well, how was the date?"

"It wasn't a date, Ritu," Neha says, with a grin on her face.

"Really, you are still holding on to that?" Ritu replies with a wink.

"Well, it was nice! I could actually talk to him," Neha says excitedly, and Ritu laughs. "Yes, I mean, the food was good too. But I kept talking to him for the whole time. I didn't feel too conscious. Didn't feel scared at all. This is a big step for me and you know, it has taken me years to reach here."

She joins Ritu on the couch. She knows there is no running away from her. Ritu will not let her sleep until she tells every detail of the meeting to her.

Neha tries to tease her and focuses on the hot chocolate in her hand. Before she can take even one sip, Ritu is already breathing down her neck.

"Don't act pricey, Neha! Out with the details!" Ritu tugs at Neha's arm.

"Stop shaking my arm, my chocolate will spill!"

"If you don't start pouring out your story immediately, this hot chocolate will be on your head," Ritu replies with a fierce look.

"I don't know where to start. I don't have the words to describe this feeling inside me. I can feel a kind of happiness that I have never felt before. It's as if someone has infused colour into a black and white painting."

"So the million dollar question – do you like him?"

"No way!" Neha replies in a tone louder than she had imagined.

From the sly smile on Ritu's face, she can only guess that she has got an awfully puzzled look on her face, and it possibly matches the confusion inside her mind right now.

"I think you need to be sure of yourself before you say no," Ritu replies calmly.

"Maybe you are right."

"You don't have to find the answer for me, Neha," she says. "You need to find the answer for yourself."

> *Say yes.*
>
> *Sometimes, love is the answer.*
>
> *We originate from love and our basic nature is love. The first feeling at birth is that of receiving unconditional love. Allow yourself to receive the love that is flowing towards you. It has the power to heal.*

9

Neha settles down on her bed for the night. She decides to pick up her diary to help sort her feelings.

Even after the best evening of my life, I am feeling empty. It feels as if something was left unsaid in the end. I should have asked him what was bothering him when he was talking to his mother. Maybe, I just was not ready to face all this. I am not feeling stuck in my past anymore; I am living in my present – all thanks to Tarun.

Maybe I don't want to know his secrets. Maybe I don't have the strength to handle them. Sometimes, it's better to live with what you have than to spoil it by trying to know things which aren't required.

When I am with Tarun, he makes me feel alive. He gives me the courage to face my demons. For the first time, I can see what my life could be if I let go of my past. I need to try. That is the least I can do.

Just as she closes her diary, she receives a call from Tarun. "I don't think I can meet you tomorrow."

"Oh! But why?"

"I've got some work to do and I would get late by the time I am done with it."

She is a bit worried by his response. He isn't himself. "Is everything okay?" she asks.

"Oh yes! I just need to take care of something," he replies hesitantly.

Just a moment ago, Neha was feeling positive about how the relationship was moving. And suddenly, his replies bring in insecurity and uncertainty.

Why does it seem that he is pulling away from me?

"I hope we will meet again very soon?" Neha questions as she tucks her diary under the pillow.

"Well, I hope so too," he says.

Neha gets this weird feeling that he is hiding something from her. "Are you sure nothing is bothering you?"

"Nothing you need to worry about right now," he replies.

"But Tarun…"

"Not now," he says, leaning in closer to the phone.

The discomfort in his voice rips through her like a tidal wave. *I want to know the reason for his discomfort. I don't want to let go of this chance to be with him. I want to be there for him if he is in trouble. Or has he decided already that I am not worthy of it?*

Tarun stares at the well-lit bar, lost in his thoughts as he thinks about Neha. The images of Neha from tonight's meeting are drifting in and out of his brain – images of Neha sitting in front of him, alive with laughter.

I don't think she has any clue about how beautiful she is. Such a pure heart. I think I am really lucky to have her in my life. While Gaurav thinks I am wasting my time with Neha, that is so not true. This is the best time I have ever had in ages. I can understand that she has some dark past, and maybe some fears, just like me.

He takes a sip of his drink as his heart keeps bringing back sweet memories of Neha. He wonders why Neha was trying to tone down her dressing style that night? She still looked so gorgeous and drew his attention even more.

But I think I screwed up big time by being rude to her, after talking to Ma. What can I do? I cannot tell her the truth. It will break her heart.

Even If I want, I cannot control my feelings for her. Oh god, I hope I am doing the right thing.

It has been two days that Neha has heard from Tarun.

As Neha finishes writing the battle of her emotions in her diary, her mobile phone buzzes to life in the otherwise quiet room. She sees Tarun's name flashing on the screen.

"Neha." The painful voice she hears is enough to make her run for the door.

"Tarun?"

"Hi! I just wanted to hear your voice."

"Are you alright?" Neha asks.

"No, I'm not fine," he replies. "Everything's so fucked up. The most awful part is I perhaps deserve it."

"Where the hell are you?" Neha asks. She has already reached her door.

"Irish Bar," he says.

"Stay there! I am coming," Neha says, disconnecting the call before he can react. *He is pushing me away just like I tried to push Ritu away initially, when she tried to help me.*

She quickly changes out of her night dress, slips on a pair of blue jeans and a t-shirt and pulls over a hoodie over her head.

She reaches the bar and notices three guys standing outside, smoking. She walks towards the door and overhears the men, talking in a slurry and loud tone, sounding really drunk. In such a situation, she would have run away, but today, she knows Tarun needs her.

She keeps her eyes on the door as she counts her steps, getting closer and closer. Only five or six more steps, she thinks.

"Hi darling, where are you going alone?" one of the men calls out, taking some wobbly steps towards her. She just keeps looking towards the door and runs to enter it.

The smell of alcohol, sweat and cigarette brings back gory memories of Dheeraj. She spots a waiter and describes how Tarun looks and asks for his whereabouts.

"Have you seen him?" Neha asks, fidgeting with her fingers.

His eyebrows pull in as his head nods toward the bathroom. "He went in there about fifteen minutes ago."

As soon as she hears his reply, she runs towards the men's room. A fat guy walks out, fastening his zip, too drunk to manage such a trivial task. She is beyond sickened, but she needs to find out if Tarun is inside. "Is there a young guy coughing like really bad in there?" she asks timidly, standing back against the wall.

His stares her top to bottom. "Yes, he's puking his guts out. I don't understand why guys drink if they can't manage their alcohol."

The second she dashes inside, she can hear Tarun coughing loudly and continuously. She sees him, bending over the wash-basin. "Can I get you some water?"

"I told you not to come here, Neha."

"I don't know why, but I just wanted to be here," she says rubbing his back.

"I don't want you to take responsibility of me," he manages to say between his breaths.

"I want to make sure you will be fine," she says. "Please walk out with me." She places his hand on the side of her back, and starts walking towards the exit.

Neha swallows the lump in her throat as she bolts upright in bed, unable to scream through her parched throat. She looks around, realizing that she is in her room in Shimla, and not in her brother's apartment.

"Fooooh!" She lets out a deep breath of air. It took several minutes for her heart to calm down. She reaches out for her diary, lying on the bedside table. She has to vent her fears out to her diary. She has written about this fear earlier too, but she knows it is her only way of taking it all out of her system.

At this point, all she can hear is her heart thumping against her ribcage. She tries to focus and start writing. Her diary is her confidant.

Why is he looking at me? Doesn't Dheeraj know that I am feeling uncomfortable?

"Now that you have told me that your brother is coming late, maybe," he says, with a really shady grin on his face. Something about his voice scares me even more than usual.

"He may come soon," I lie as I see Dheeraj staring at me.

Dheeraj comes closer to me on the couch. Too close. He moves one of his arms behind my back. I am scared to death as he starts moving his hand slowly on my back.

Maybe he is just comforting me, as my brother isn't here. The moment I try to convince myself that he wasn't being cheap, he moves his other hand on my bare leg under my skirt. He slowly lifts up the skirt and moves his hand further up. I freeze with fear and stare at him.

"Oh, I am sorry if you didn't like it," he fakes an apology.

My entire body is shivering with fear; I just can't control it. "I think I should go to Manish's room and sleep," I manage to say.

He's still ogling at me in the same repulsive, degrading way he always used to – like I'm not a living being, but instead an appealing piece of meat he can't hold himself to dig into.

My heart sinks in absolute horror as he locks my hands on the couch and gets on top of me with that nasty smirk of his.

Oh god! This can't be happening!

Just as Neha closes her diary and begins to cry, Ritu walks in and hugs her tightly.

"May you rot in hell, Dheeraj," Neha cries, trembling and hugging Ritu tightly. "Fuck you!"

"Dheeraj is your past. He is no longer a part of your life, Neha," Ritu says as Neha continues to cry. "I know he was an asshole, but you are safe here with me. And no one is going to hurt you now."

Neha continues to sob with shaky, unsteady breaths and Ritu realizes what's going on in Neha's heart. She is worried if Tarun would turn out to be the same.

"Tarun is a great guy, and not one bit like Dheeraj," she says, her voice composed and comforting as she runs a hand slowly through Neha's hair. "Have faith, Neha. You should give him a chance!"

"Dheeraj still controls my life, after so many years, and I hate him for that. I just hate him more than anyone else in the world."

Ritu tightens her embrace and pats Neha on the back to soothe her fears.

Neha keeps crying for a long time before she falls asleep in Ritu's arms. The next things she remembers is her alarm clock ringing. She wakes up with an awfully stiff neck. She's lying on Ritu's lap, with Ritu stroking Neha's hair like an elder sister would.

"Are you feeling better, Neha?" Ritu murmurs. Neha nods uncomfortably and gets up to switch off the alarm.

"It's morning and you stayed awake the whole night, Ritu? For me?"

"Right now, you don't have to worry about me," she replies. "The good thing is that you are feeling alright now." Ritu smiles.

"I don't know how you will manage classes today, Ritu. You haven't slept all night," Neha says with a sense of guilt.

"I had to choose between a few sleepy classes versus my best friend's comfort. The decision was pretty simple."

"I don't really deserve someone like you, Ritu. You're an angel." Neha cannot help but feel grateful for Ritu being with her.

"You were there for me too, Neha," she says feebly, her voice cracking. "When my parents went away. I promised myself to be there for you. That's what true friends are for, right?"

She grabs Ritu and pulls her into a long, tight hug. "Yes, of course. You are right."

A warm feeling overwhelms Ritu as she Neha hugs her. She remembers her mother's last words, "Princess, one day you'll find someone who will love you like your father and I do. Remember to guard your heart, and don't just let anyone in. But, once you have let someone in, take good care of that person, in both good and bad times. To love strongly is a great thing. To be loved just as strongly in return, that is a miracle in itself."

> "*Create a tight inner circle of true friends, who connect with your true self. They see you at your worst. They know when to allow you to break down and cry and let it all out. And they know when to set you straight.*
>
> *This practice has helped me a lot. My friends have lifted me up in tough times. They have helped me become who I am today. They are a part of me and I am a part of them. This kind of friendship is what will make your world a beautiful place.*"

10

It was two days later that she saw Tarun again in the college. Neha sat in class looking at him, realizing with every passing moment that something about Tarun didn't seem right. He seemed to be in pain.

What she didn't know was that the previous night, he had gone back to the same bar and knocked the guts out of the guys who had troubled Neha. He wanted to make sure they never bother her again. He hated bullies and didn't want to give them another chance to take away someone really important to him. Someone like Neha.

He knows that she is sitting next to him, but he is in a really bad shape. He forces his eyes on to the notebook and tries to clumsily write with his left hand.

"Left hand?" Neha looks at him and wonders.

He turns around and she sees that his right hand is covered in a thick crepe bandage. He winces in pain as he moves it slowly to place it on the table for support.

For the remaining lecture, she does not hear a word of what professor says. Her eyes lock onto Tarun, observing as he clumsily tries to write with his left hand with dreadful sadness. He can feel Neha's eyes boring into him and is thinking of answers to her expected questions.

After the class is over, the moment Neha decides to ask him about his injury, the girl sitting on his other side walks up to him and asks, "Hey Tarun! What happened? Did you get into a fight?"

"Nothing," he says in an uninterested voice.

"Maybe if you share your pain with me, it may lessen a bit," Priya tries to flirt with him.

Neha glares at her and then, unknowingly sends a glare at Tarun's way. Tarun backs away from Priya and then calmly says, "Sorry Priya, there is nothing to tell. I need to go right now, Neha is waiting for me."

Neha's stomach is in her throat. *Is he just saying that because he is trying to get away from that flirtatious Priya, or because he genuinely wants to come and meet me?*

Tarun steps towards Neha, as Priya slinks off his desk. "Tarun?"

He motions her to walk with him and they both step out of the campus. She follows Tarun to wherever he is heading. He stops at a shop and buys an ice pack. Resuming the walk, he takes up a small dirt road which she does not recognize. But she trusts him and keeps walking until he reaches a green iron bench. He gestures to Neha to take a seat.

She quietly sits down next to him. She looks around and realizes that she is directly facing the sky, and the view in front of her is an amazing orange glow with hints of purple and pink painting the sky. Down below is thickly wooded forest creating a green carpet as far as she can see.

He removes the crepe bandage and holds the ice pack on top of his right hand. It looks like he's in real pain, both physically and emotionally.

They sit together for a few minutes with barely a word passing between them.

"I usually come and sit here when I am a bit low," he breaks the silence.

"Is it okay if I ask what happened to your hand?" says Neha in a timid voice.

Hearing her words doesn't seem to change his expression. He is in so much pain that his hands are shaking. "I just hurt my hand a bit," he finally manages to say.

"That's not a little bit," Neha almost screams.

This is not a normal reaction from Neha. She is usually very passive and does not fight tooth and nail. But somehow, she is not able to see Tarun in pain and wants to help.

"I'm okay, Neha." Tarun clears his throat, a scowl crossing his face.

"Stop hiding your pain and show me your hand!" she snaps, glaring angrily at him.

He finally puts his hand forward and removes the ice pack.

"That must have been some serious accident," Neha says, as she gently holds his swollen hand. "Are you able to move your fingers? Rotate your wrist?"

When he doesn't say anything, she takes the call. "That's it! Stand up! I'm taking you to a doctor."

"It's just a minor injury, Neha!"

"Can't you see? It's not a minor injury. It is pretty evident that you have broken a bone!" Neha shouts at him.

Tarun does not know what to say. He stares at Neha and words do not come to him. Neha lets her eyes fall to the floor and says nothing. She is uncertain if she has the right to shout at him?

"I am used to getting my bones broken. I will be fine," he says innocently.

"It might be normal for you, but it isn't for me," she huffs. "This isn't a discussion; we are going to the clinic."

Tarun realizes that she is not going to agree. "Okay, you win. I will come," he finally gives in. "But where?"

"I have seen a sign-board of Shimla Bone and Joint Centre on the Cart Road, just opposite the bus terminal."

"Have you been there?"

"No, not really, but I think it's better to go there than just leave your broken thumb with your ice pack." Her concern for him is all over her face.

The night sky is full of stars and the crescent moon shines. While it only took the doctor around fifty minutes to set a cast on Tarun's hand, but they still had to wait a while; there were a lot of patients queued up before them.

"I think the pain killer he gave me was really potent. I am feeling a bit dizzy," Tarun says, as they walk towards his apartment.

"Don't worry, it's more important to subdue the pain than to keep you awake," she says, holding his arm over her shoulder for support.

"Watch out for that rock," she says as she guides him, slowly but steadily.

It takes them more than forty minutes to reach his apartment and another fifteen minutes for him to search for the key. He is too groggy and is unable to figure out where he had kept the key in the morning.

Even when he finally finds his keys, he keeps dropping them and cannot fit it into the keyhole. Neha takes the key from him, unlocks the door and then, sighs happily as they can now be in a much warmer environment as compared the blazing cold outside.

"Can I get you anything from the kitchen?" Neha asks him after helping him sit on the couch.

"Ya! A beer might help."

Neha lets out a laugh. "Are you serious? It's freezing cold and you just had a painkiller. Sorry, beer isn't possible."

Tarun lets out a sigh.

"I can make you some good coffee; that can keep you warm," Neha offers.

Before Tarun can answer, she walks off to the kitchen.

"Have you ever been to Embassy Cafe?"

"Of course, who wouldn't have gone there!"

"Oh I just love that place. In fact, the couple that runs it actually taught me how to make good coffee."

"Really?"

"Yes! I am not making it up. Once I had coffee at their place and I just asked them the recipe. They were sweet enough to tell me."

"That coffee is to die for! And their carrot cake too," Tarun says, with a lingering smile.

"Well, I can't make a carrot cake right now, but coffee, I will."

Neha turns around and searches through the small kitchen and pulls out coffee, sugar, a large pan, a long spoon and some milk. Oh yes, a mug!

She is feeling a bit hungry too, so she walks over to the refrigerator to find something for herself. A box of strawberries sitting on the first tray in the refrigerator catches her attention immediately. *He has strawberries. And they are all mine,* Neha thinks elatedly.

Neha picks up the coffee mug in one hand and the box of strawberries in the other. She walks up to Tarun and sits down next to him on the couch. She offers him the coffee and he grabs it hastily.

He looks at the frothy coffee in front of him and is unable to believe that it is home-made. It smells different too, though he isn't able to figure out the secret ingredient.

He takes a sip and is mesmerized by the deliciousness. "I have never had such coffee in my life."

"I am glad you like it," Neha beams with happiness.

"What have you put in it?"

"Well, coffee, milk and sugar! What else?" She giggles at the question.

"No, it tastes yummy and smells so different."

"Okay, I'll give you my secret recipe. I sprinkled a bit of chocolate powder and cinnamon on top of it."

"Hmm… Amazing. I am sure even if I put all these together, I will never be able to make such mind-blowing coffee."

"Enough about the coffee." She holds up the box of strawberries, and asks, "Can I have these?"

"Well that's a big box, you may have to stay for some time to finish it," he says.

"Well I plan to stay here, until you want me to stay,"

"That's great. I do need some good company as Gaurav is out drinking with some guys," he says.

Neha looks at his right hand, which seems to be in a much better state. The swelling has also diminished.

"Tarun?" she asks in her softest, sweetest voice.

"I got angry, and hurt myself," he says before she can ask him anything. "That's all I can tell you," he says.

Although, she knows something is not right, she never expected this. She is shocked that he knew what she was going to say. Tarun gets up from the couch and walks up to a picture on the wall; Neha follows him.

Neha smiles at seeing the younger, cuter version of Tarun. A gorgeous little girl is standing right next to him.

Then, he looks at the adjacent picture and keeps staring at it. "This is my family," Tarun approaches the subject lightly. "This is my broken family," he says

His father is really tall, almost 6.5 feet, wearing a police uniform, and has a thick mustache and a scruffy beard. Most of Tarun's features seem to be inherited from his beautiful mother. She is slim and attractive, with short but thick jet black hair curling at her shoulders and a rounded nose. He isn't like his father at all.

"Doesn't look broken to me. It looks like one of the best family portraits I have ever seen," she says.

"Well, that was the purpose of the photograph," he says, with his nose and lips wrinkled.

"I am not sure if I am following this," she says, in a confused tone.

"Each one of us was either beaten or threatened before going to the photo studio," he says, with a sad look on his face.

Neha manages to push back the tears that were building up in her eyes. She holds his hand warmly and gives it a gentle squeeze as he looks intently at the family portrait. He turns to look at her and releases the breath he has been holding.

"Remember I had told you that I am used to broken bones." He stops abruptly, unsure if he can share his dark secrets any further, but Neha comes close to him and holds his hands.

"You can trust me, Tarun," she says.

"My father used to beat me when I was a child," he says, a lump forming in his throat. "He has broken numerous bones over the years, and that is the reason I never want to see him again."

Neha takes a step forward and hugs him. She knows that he really needs her to hold him right now. Neha strokes his back to comfort him and can feel the deep breaths.

"I don't ever want to go back home," he says. "And I have no one to look forward to meeting in that house."

She finally let go of him to ask, "What about the girl in that picture?" She points out to the adjacent picture. "Wouldn't you want to meet her?" She sees tears pooling in his eyes, and the last thing she wanted to do was hurt him, but she knows she has accidentally done it.

"I wish I could meet her, Neha," his head snaps up. "But I can't." Tarun looks right into her eyes, with the fear of being judged and rejected. Neha can relate to the pain in his eyes. She remembers exactly how she felt when she told her dark secrets to Ritu.

"She was my best friend, Aditi. I believed we were invincible, and I learned the hard way that we're not. Now, I'm paying for it."

"Is that the reason that you are in Shimla?"

"Yes, one of the reasons," he says.

"Then, what about Aditi?"

"When I was fourteen, my best friend Aditi got badly hurt because of me!" he manages to say.

"What?"

"I couldn't protect her from my alcoholic father," he says with his teeth clenched.

"What did your father do?"

"Aditi tried to protect my mother from this man's mad rage, and he beat her so much that she fell down unconscious. I tried to protect her, but I was late. By the time, I tried to open my door, it was already too late. I realized the door was locked from outside. I jumped out of the window and ran to the front door."

"And…" Neha's breath was caught in her throat.

"When I reached, I saw Aditi lying unconscious on the floor."

"Was she alright later?"

"I am not sure. When I went to her place to check on her, the house was locked. The family had packed up and left town. My father was an ex-cop and most people feared him and his influential contacts. After all that happened, her family probably did the right thing to keep her safe."

She hesitantly rests her hand on his shoulder and gives it a gentle squeeze. "You tried, how is it your fault? You have to forgive yourself." Neha hugs him closely to calm him down, but it doesn't simmer him down.

"It's my mistake that she was hurt. And I live with this guilt every second." The tone of his voice is icy and lifeless as he completes his sentence, and he pulls away from her and moves back to the sofa.

"How long back did you have your last painkiller tablet?" Neha asks, trying to change the topic to bring him out of his dark memories.

"Almost four-and-a-half hours ago," he replies, looking up at the wall clock with his anger-filled eyes.

"It's time for you to have the next one," she says.

Tarun gulps it down with his coffee, which has now gone cold, and Neha comes and sits next to him on the couch.

"I am really sorry, Tarun. I didn't mean to hurt you," she says awkwardly.

"It's okay," he replies. "I had to tell you how wrecked I am."

"You're definitely not a wreck!" Neha objects, but when he continues to repeat it, Neha changes the subject.

"Here, have a strawberry!" she says, offering him from the box.

"I like strawberries," he says, shutting his eyes and leaning his head on the arm of the sofa. The strong painkiller is showing its effect; he is sleepy.

"Neha?" Tarun murmurs in a sleepy voice.

"Yeah?"

"We are quite similar, aren't we?"

Neha knows he is right. In fact, that's the reason she finds trusting him easier. "Maybe we are," she says, a little too late. Tarun is already asleep.

Tarun sleeps peacefully in front of her. Neha cannot help but stare at him. He is the first guy in a long time that she has seen so closely or ever felt attracted to.

Neha lovingly brushes his hair away from his face and looks at the extensive scar running along his jaw. She reaches out apprehensively and runs a finger along it gently. It's a crooked line, like a barb wire. She notices a few more scars on his neck and the part of his chest that she can see.

"Your father hit you a lot," Neha says, under her breath as she reaches out and gently moves her hand in his thick hair.

You are so lonely, and in pain. Yes, you are just like me, full of scars. The only difference is that you have visible scars and I have a deep scar in my heart which no one can see or feel. But you can feel it. And so can I. Maybe, two broken hearts can heal each other.

> "*When I am having a difficult time, I reach out to my friends, the ones with a strong personality, the ones that have a story to tell and truly know who they are because that story has shaped them. The ones who will stand by me when I need them and would support me without question... not to forget, who genuinely want the best for me. The soft-hearted, but strong-minded.*"

11

The morning sunlight, seeping in from the window, stabs Tarun's eyes. He tries to sit up slowly, but his head is throbbing with pain. Thoughts of Neha sitting right next to him are so fresh that he can barely determine whether it was real or he was hallucinating. He grabs the water bottle from the center table while he tries to scan the room.

He grips his head between his hands to steady himself, but then a pillow comes flying. It hits him on the head and the water bottle slips from his hand.

His gaze darts around to see Gaurav sprawled on the next couch, sipping his tea.

"Dude? What did you smoke up last night?" says Gaurav.

"Huh?" Tarun replies as he runs a hand through his hair.

"Just try to relax, man!" says Gaurav. "I heard you broke bones of some bullies again!"

"Shhh… just keep it low. Don't tell Neha about it."

"Dude! I haven't told anybody, and if you don't want, I won't tell anyone."

Tarun slumps back into the couch and rests his head back. He presses the heels of his hands on his eyes. "I feel like a mess."

"You look like it too, bro," says Gaurav, shaking his head. "Here, have some tea!" He pours half the tea from his cup to an empty one.

Tarun draws in a deep breath and glances at the wall clock. "Oh shit! I had to submit my project in the morning!"

"Don't' worry. Your teacher has been informed," says Gaurav, in a calm and composed tone. "He knows you have a broken thumb and can't make it today."

"Gaurav! He is going to kill me!" Tarun sits up, rubbing the back of his neck in an attempt to chase away the tension that had gathered in the muscles, to shake off the anxiety that clung like decay.

"Just relax and have some food! You need to fill your stomach." He passed on a plate, with some buttered toasted bread.

"And what about the classes today?"

"Neha is making notes for the common subjects and she is going to take the rest of the notes from someone in your class. She called your teacher and requested time extension on medical grounds," he reveals.

Tarun gazes expressionlessly at him, and then suddenly, the previous night comes whooshing back to him.

Neha was with me all night. I actually slept on the couch as she moved her fingers in my hair. Wait, did she? He looks at the cask on his hand and in a blur, Neha's face rushes through his mind. He remembers how she took care of him all night.

A surge of worry flows over him as he recalls telling Neha about his dark past. *I told her everything that I had buried away from the world. I can't believe I told her about Aditi and my alcoholic father.*

New fears clutter his mind, as he is not sure if Neha would like to stay friends with a broken guy like him. Embarrassment rushes up his spine and settles in the back of his neck. He looks down and massages the tense muscles.

"Did Neha tell you anything about last night?" Tarun asks Gaurav.

"Yes, she told me she forced you to go to a doctor and then about the heavy painkillers that you had to take."

"That's all?"

"Why? Is there more?" Gaurav studies him, his expression like that of a nosey neighbour.

"I…uh…" Tarun didn't know what to say or how to respond.

"You should have told me about those guys. I could have come with you to beat them up!" Gaurav frowns.

"It's my redemption. I've got to do this alone."

"What redemption? Why are you talking like a Bollywood hero – *yeh meri jung hai, main he ladunga.*"

Tarun struggles to find a valid explanation, but can't think of any.

"And here, all this while, I was thinking Neha was the crazy one!"

Dragging a hand through his hair, Tarun releases a controlled breath. He glances up at Gaurav and wishes to say something.

"You did not want any help from me, but you let Neha help you?"Gaurav cut his narrowed eyes towards Tarun.

"She forced me to go to the clinic." Tarun manages to say, looking down at the box of strawberries still sitting on the table. His guilt magnifies as Gaurav keeps staring at him.

Tarun's nerves ramp up what feels like a hundred notches when he hears a knock on the front door. A minute later, Neha walks in. "Hi, I'm back!" she chirps from the door. She walks over to him with a smile and keeps his project papers on the table. She plops herself on the sofa next to him.

"That's a lot of work!" exclaims Gaurav as he gazes at the huge stack of work.

"I hope it isn't as cumbersome as it appears to be," Tarun answers as he eyes the tower of papers. He wonders how he will do all this work with a broken hand.

"How will you do this with a broken hand?" Neha says, as if she has read his mind.

"Maybe I can try and do it with my left hand."

Gaurav laughs humourlessly. "You can't be serious, dude!"

Tarun ignores Gaurav's comment and picks up the first project sheet from the table, forcing a pen in his left hand. He tries to write the answer to the first question and realizes that his handwriting is even worse than the doctor's prescription which he got last night. Totally illegible!

Gaurav leans forward and looks at the sheet. "That certainly is awesome. In case you are attempting to write in Chinese."

Tarun pauses, but does not look his way. "I think I can manage it," Tarun says stubbornly.

Inching closer, Neha holds his hand and stops him from writing any further. "I have classes during the day, but I can see you in the evening and help you with this." Her expression is sweet and caring.

Tarun's stony resolve begins to waver with the warmth of her hand and the concern that laces her voice. He doesn't want to waste her time doing his project work, but he is elated that she wants to still spend time with him even after knowing of his dark secrets.

"I am sure you have better things to do," Tarun scrubs his hand over his weary face, forcing the air from his lungs and dropping the subject.

"Come on! It's not a big thing," Neha says. "I would love to do it."

"Are you sure?"

"Maybe, you can pay me in strawberries and hot chocolate," she says sweetly.

"If you're up for helping me with my assignment," Tarun says, "then I am totally ready for making hot chocolate for you!"

"That's great!" She smiles and turns excitedly towards the door. "I will finish all my classes and then talk to you, okay?"

"That sounds like a plan!" Tarun replies, with a broad smile on his face as he catches Gaurav, making faces at him out of the corner of his eye.

Just as Neha is about to close the door behind her, Tarun calls out, "Neha?"

"Yes?"

She turns around slowly and Tarun is dumbstruck with her beauty. *I wish I could kiss you right now,* he thinks. "Thanks for everything," Tarun stammers, instead.

"I should be the one to thank you. I heard someone mysteriously beat those boys at the pub."

"Who? What boys?" Tarun tries to pretend he doesn't understand.

She looks at his cask, her smile affectionate and intimate.

She looks up at the flash of lightning that blankets the evening sky as she walks out of the college campus towards Tarun's apartment. It's a thirty-minute walk at least, and the cold weather isn't helping. Within no time, her toes and hands are numb, and there's still a long way to go.

Fatigue and cold slow her feet, but she continues walking in excitement. "I am excited about doing someone else's homework!" She laughs. Deep down her heart, she knows this someone has been the only blip of happiness in a life full of pain.

"Oh god, it's so cold. I am dying to be in the warm apartment right next to Tarun. And yes, the hot chocolate might help too."

The moment she rings the doorbell, the door opens as if Tarun was already eagerly waiting for her.

"Hi Neha!" he hugs her and invites her in. "Thanks for all your help. You know, I hate assignments, or for that matter, anything to do with studies." He chuckles.

Neha feels warm in his embrace, and manages to say, "It's not a big deal." She smiles and walks into the house to take off her moist shoes and jacket. She looks at the heater and feels glad that it's much warmer inside.

Tarun walks over to the couch and slowly sits on it, looking at the never-ending bundles of assignments waiting to kick his ass.

There are two mugs of steaming hot chocolate on the table and Neha can't help but smile at his sweet gesture. She walks and sits on the couch next to him.

"You can dictate the answer if I get stuck, does that work?"

Tarun nods and rubs his hand over his chin.

"But I usually don't get stuck," she replies, bringing in a smile on his confused face.

She grabs a blue pen and starts the assignment.

Page after page flies by in silence, with Tarun trying to answer in bits, although Neha already knows all the answers. Neha feels warm and content as she sits next to him. She wonders how much she has overcome her fears in just three weeks. She used to be a nervous wreck around guys, and now she is actually making an effort to be close to him.

"You have been working continuously for pretty long. Want to take a break?" Tarun asks and Neha quickly tosses away the stack of papers, stretching out her aching limbs.

"I think I can do some more," she replies with a smile on her face. Although she is tired from the work, she wants to be with him. She likes being with him. She has never felt this way,– warm and safe. She is unable to actually explain the feeling to herself. She feels good with Ritu too, but this is just different.

She moves her arm forward to pick a text book from the table, Tarun does the same, and her hand lands on top of his. It is as if time stops. She continues to look into his eyes as they sit there, hand on hand.

A moment later, Tarun realizes what has just happened, so he pulls his hand away. But somehow, Neha can still feel the warmth of his touch. Now that it isn't there, she wants it back.

Silence seizes as they both look away from each other, focusing on the paper in their hand, clearly not reading it.

In just those few seconds, Tarun felt something he'd never felt before. He couldn't resist the urge to seek her out. He watches Neha avert her gaze. He can catch glimpses of her round cheeks, her rosy pink skin, and her dark red lips. He involuntarily continues to look at her, drawn for the first time in his life. This was different than what he had ever felt before. Something, he didn't entirely understand.

Neha tries to concentrate on the assignment at hand. She lets her right arm drop to her side, sitting on the couch. She side-glances stealthily and watches her hand inch toward his, as if in slow motion. Her pulse pounds so piercingly in her head that it's almost deafening as her fingers enfold slowly around his.

For a second, she thinks that he's going to pull away from her, but then his fingers close around hers.

"You okay?" he asks, his voice full of worry and doubt.

Neha nods and smiles shyly. "I'm trying to be," Neha whispers. Confusion and emotions that she doesn't know how to deal with plow through her senses.

Tarun is just as afraid as she is, and maybe that's the reason she feels safe with him.

Neha really wants to trust him. Not just because she feels safe with him, but because he makes her feel the way she has never felt before. He makes butterflies flutter in her stomach and her heart pound. She feels special.

Tarun tries to pull his hand from her, worried that she may not be okay with it. But, Neha grabs his hand even more tightly. "No, I don't want to let go." She is sure.

He squeezes her hand softly. "Even I don't want this moment to end." He smiles back.

His eyes are welcoming and compassionate, and as he smiles at her, she feels like she could just melt into him. She squeezes his hand back and her uneasiness disappears away. Something extraordinary and pleasing, though still frightening and new, is taking over. She is not sure what she is feeling, but she likes it.

"Err…so," Tarun stammers as he tears his gaze away from Neha.

Neha realizes that she has been so lost in him that she has forgotten about the assignment. "I think we were on answer four. Let's try and finish this. Shall we?"

Neha looks at her hand; her fingers are still intertwined with his. "You know, even I can't write with my left hand," Neha says. "If we have to finish the assignment, then you have to let go of my hand."

"Later?" he says abruptly, and Neha gapes back at him blankly.

"Sorry?"

"This is…awkward," he stutters, feeling humiliated. "Well, when we're done with this assignment, can we?"

She smiles and nods her head up and down, and she leans against his shoulder to feel the warmth of his body. They are almost cuddling each other now and when she turns to look at him, her lips brush against his. She wants to kiss him, but is really afraid it will spiral her back to her past.

Tarun can feel her spirit pulsing against him, wrapping and coiling around him, while she is withdrawing at the same time. He knows he cannot escape Neha any more that she can escape him.

"Neha..." Slowly, he untwines their fingers and moves a bit forward to hold her face between his hands.

Neha can feel his warm and trembling hands against her cheeks. Every bit of her was racing – her nerves, her heart, her mind.

Leaning back, he trails his fingertips down the side of her face. She smiles as he traces them along the line of her lips. Her skin tingles and she is unable to make sense of how someone can make her feel this way.

"You are so beautiful. Do you know that?"

Her heart hums with joy and she aches to feel more of his touch. Locks of hair fall around her face when she leans in. Though he reaches up with the intention of brushing her hair back, he can't stop himself from winding his fingers through the black waves.

He hovers two inches from her face, wavering, rocking in indecision, before he presses his lips to hers. The close-mouthed kiss feels innocent, the single most intimate moment they have ever shared with anyone. They linger, breathing into each other, their hands shaking and pulses thundering.

Tarun is surprised with the loss of contact when she suddenly pulls away. Visible panic wells in her, that old sadness darkening her face when she touches her fingertips to her lips. The pain in her eyes is visible as dark memories drag her to her worst nightmares. Her fear is screaming for her to get out of this situation, but her heart is imploring her to overcome this fear and stay.

"What happened?" says Tarun inaudibly.

Oh for god's sake, kiss him again! pleads her heart and her body, begging her to overlook the cloud of fear looming over her.

"Are you alright?"

I've had enough. I'm tired of being scared and I don't want him to give me an excuse to run away. Neha tries to make up her mind.

Before he can realize what's happening and before her nightmares can override her senses, she pushes herself back across the sofa. She takes his face in her hands and kisses him hard, in a way that tells him that she is sure about this. Their mouths move slowly, steadily building intensity.

Tarun kisses her back, softly plucking at her lower lip as he tastes her sweetness. Then, he pulls her close to him and hugs her warmly.

His warm arms around her, his strong chest pressing against hers. Just when she feels like she could die and go to heaven, the gates of hell open up and she remembers her darkest hours with Dheeraj.

"No Dheeraj, stay away!" I was crying.

"Oh my baby, you should know this. I find you very hot, I always have. I always used to keep looking at you when I came to your place to meet your brother. I used to find you very cute and kept trying to get an opportunity to spend time with you." His large hands tightened around my hands.

"I am just a kid, Dheeraj!" I try to put across a simple fact, hoping he would understand and let me go. I can smell alcohol in his breath and am petrified.

Oh god, please don't let this happen. Please.

"I know you like me. You always looked at me so longingly," he continues to say things which don't make sense. The way he kept looking at me, with lecherous eyes, I hated him.

Dheeraj pushed me towards the bed and then pounced on me.

"Leave me! Let me go!"

He pressed my body flat onto the cold bed with his, breathing into my ear, "I know you want me too, baby." He dug his fingers into my sides and the pain made me gasp .

No. This can't be happening to me.

I squeezed my eyes shut as tears raced down my face. I released a weighty breath, my bare chest palpitating with tremors. I was so afraid that I thought I was paralyzed with it. He lies on top of me and does what he shouldn't have.

"Just leave me. For god's sake, leave me!" Neha shrieks, wiggling out of Tarun's hold and pushing him away.

"Neha, what happened?" he asks shocked, pulling his hands back.

She moves back from him, but the triggered memory is already fading from her mind. She realizes she isn't with Dheeraj. *I am sure he thinks I am crazy.*

"I can't do this." Neha whimpers, trying to hold back her tears. "I mean, I really want to, but I am unable to!"

"I understand," replies Tarun, his voice composed and supportive. *I wish I could erase these dark memories and set her free.*

She thinks. *I know Tarun is trying his best to be patient with me, but what can I do, I am completely shattered from inside. I don't deserve a guy like him.*

"I need to go," Neha announces, jumping up from the sofa. She stomps out of the door without saying a word, heading straight to her apartment. Tarun follows, but doesn't know what to say to her.

Neha keeps running blindly, until she reaches the door of her apartment and bursts inside.

"Ritu! Ritu! Where are you?" She looks around the apartment for her. Neha pushes open the door to Ritu's room.

"Hey! Actually? Can it wait until we finish the movie?" says Ritu.

"We?" Neha's jaw drops as she sees Ritu cuddled up next to Gaurav with a bowl of popcorn, some romantic movie playing on the television. She has no words, her throat is thick with emotions.

"Oh I didn't know. I am sorry to barge in like this," she manages to say as humiliation bites at her feet.

She leaves Ritu and Gaurav to their movie date and races to her bedroom. The only possible way to vent out her emotions is her diary. She locks the door behind her and grabs her diary from beneath the pillow to write her heart out.

> *Letting go is about accepting what is happening right now and not worrying about what happened in the past. The more we can detach our identity from our thoughts, the easier letting go becomes.*
>
> *What we decide to do with our thoughts is what can either make or break us.*

12

Neha turns around to see some girl sitting on Tarun's usual seat. She looks around, hoping that he is sitting somewhere else. But to her dismay, he isn't in class. He has not come to college for the second day in a row and Neha wonders what has happened.

Since the day she ran away from his apartment, she hasn't spoken to Tarun. Not that he hasn't called; he has. Twice. But she hasn't taken his calls. She feels so humiliated by what she did that she just cannot sum up the strength to talk to him.

After not seeing him for two days, she misses his presence way too much and calls him. This time too, he doesn't answer her call too.

"Okay students! Let's get started where we left off last time – chapter ten," calls out the professor. "Any questions about the chapter we discussed yesterday?"

The remaining lecture passes by in a haze. Tarun's absence occupies her mind and everything the professor says hovers above her head without registering.

She knows that the right thing to do is to concentrate on the lecture, but her mind keeps going back to Tarun. She wants to run back to him and be close to him. But she is afraid that she has scared him away by acting like a wierdo when they kissed.

Her heart and mind are completely occupied with thoughts of Tarun. The day flies away meaninglessly as she attends worthless classes with no possible learning. *This can't go on forever. I need to talk to him.*

She skips the last class and walks out of the campus with a strong resolution to meet Tarun. The afternoon sky has darkened, the air is thick with clouds hovering in the sky.

With every step her heart is drumming like it wants to jump out of her. She continues walking, lost in her thoughts, fighting her past and present.

She stops dead, in her tracks at the corner of the hillside road as her worried, scared mind conjures up an image of Dheeraj in front of her eyes. The cold wind rocks her as she stands at the small wooden fence between her and the valley. She stares deep down into the blackness below. She can hear the sound of a waterfall hitting somewhere far below on the rocks. She remembers having read in a newspaper recently that they're going to build a new tall steel railing here because of increasing cases of suicide.

All this suffering can be over, all the dark memories can be erased. All I need to do is jump from here and be I can be free – even from Dheeraj.

She leans on the railing, listening to the bird sounds and the wind moving through the trees. The sound of a motorcycle horn brings her back to her senses and she realizes where she is standing.

"If I even think about this, I will lose Tarun," she snaps back to her senses. "If I jump, Dheeraj will win again. I won't let him win and take Tarun away from me."

She breaks free from her chilling, suicidal trance and hurries across the bridge. She doesn't understand what just came over her, and she is too scared to think about it.

Her heart jumps up a beat as she lifts her head only slightly, surprised to find Tarun standing there. He is leaning against the streetlamp with his arms crossed and a shawl wrapped around his cast like a glove.

He looks so peaceful standing there, his arms crossed against his waist as he stares out into the vastness of the valley.

Tarun feels someone's eyes on him and turns to catch her eyes, her breath catching at the unguarded desire she sees there. It was at that very moment she realizes she is starving for him. She wants her heart to pound with life like she knew it would, should their lips meet.

Neha swallows hard, the sound echoing in her ears, so loud, she is sure it's bouncing off the valley for everyone to hear.

Neha tries to silence the voice in her head that is urging her to turn and go, leaving Tarun to follow if he chooses. Instead, she steps closer to the eyes that beckon, unable to resist any longer. Their eyes lock again, then Neha spreads her arms to welcome him and he steps tentatively towards her and hugs her.

They hug each other, not saying a word.

"Neha?" He pulls away a bit.

"Yes?"

"I just wanted to say that I am really sorry," he manages to say.

"Huh?"

"I shouldn't have pushed you into a kiss."

She is shocked. All this while she has been thinking that he must be mad at her.

Instead he is apologizing to me? Doesn't he remember that I was the one who kissed him first?

"Tarun, I am going to say something and you have to trust me on it, okay?" she tells him as she moves back close to him. "It wasn't your mistake at all. In fact, I am surprised that you are apologizing for it. You have to believe me. It wasn't you!"

"What was the reason then? I want to know," he asks firmly. She stands there, as unmoving as the mountains around them. "I want to know what's bothering you. Please, Neha! Let me help you."

"Just take my word; it has nothing to do with you! All I ask from you is a lot of patience to just be with me," she replies, almost pleading "I don't want you to go away from me."

He smiles warmly and replies, "I am with you."

"Are you up for some hot chocolate?" she asks, changing the subject.

Tarun smiles, excitement showing in his eyes. "My place or yours?" He smirks.

"My place," Neha answers. "But before that, I need to finish what I started."

Neha moves into Tarun's arms, sliding her own over his shoulders. She presses her body tightly against Tarun, her eyes closes as her mouth opens to the kiss. She presses her lips onto Tarun's, kissing them hard.

She knew if she didn't do it now, they never would.

Tarun's black eyes were drawing her close, pulling her in, kissing her deeply.

She continues to kiss him slowly, breathing deeply, remembering the unique smell of Tarun from the other night. Was it perfume or simply the sweet smell of cedars and the mountains? It was all so new to her, this attraction. For the first time in her life, she really wanted this.

When they manage to pull away, with great difficulty, they can't help but smile.

"So, to the hot chocolate?" Neha she says, offering her hand.

He takes it, then grabs her in a bear hug. Together, they walk hand in hand the rest of the way toward Neha's apartment.

Ritu and Gaurav are talking merrily with two glasses of wine when they come in through the front door. Ritu waves cheerfully to Tarun, jumps up and gives him a hug. She rattles on excitedly at him and pulls him over to the couch to talk, and Neha walks to the kitchen to make hot chocolate.

"Didn't expect to see you here, Tarun!" exclaims Gaurav. Tarun shrugs. "What the hell's going on?" Gaurav asks as he perches on the edge of the couch, crossing his feet at the ankles.

Tarun and Neha momentarily look at each other, and then in unison answer, "Nothing."

Neha blushes and Ritu laughs. She knows Neha so well that she doesn't have to say anything else. She can actually read Neha's mind and by now, knows everything. She can't wait to get Neha alone. Oh, the teasing would be merciless.

Ritu sits down beside Gaurav and kisses his cheek as he cuddles her into his arms.

"Wow. What's going on between you two?"

"Nothing!" Ritu gives the same reply with a wide grin on her face.

"But I thought you weren't into Gaurav like that?" Neha tries to tease her.

"But now I am," she says, "I have decided to move on from my past and enjoy my present which looks really delicious to me," she says as she looks at Gaurav.

"Eww, get a room!" Neha says, as she winks at Ritu. The smile she sees on Ritu's face tells Neha how happy she is to find true love.

Neha has just finished her last lecture and is in the corridor. Her mobile buzzes to life and she sees Tarun's face on the screen. A broad smile spreads across her face.

She wonders how she transformed from a scared victim to a truly romantic person who was now ready to accept love and life. All thanks to Tarun and Ritu.

"Hey! I just finished my classes," she stutters. She ran her hand through her hair and then down her face. *Why do I get so conscious when I speak to him? It's like I want to say a lot, but the words just disappear. I want to tell him so many things, but I just can't speak!*

"Oh, okay yes," he is equally nervous. "I just wanted to check if you'd be willing to go out with me tonight." He says in one breath and pauses.

"I would love to go out with you!" Neha blurts out eagerly, her heart jumping leaps and bounds inside her. "But where?"

""The Footloose discotheque has a Salsa night tonight."

"Oh! I got two left feet. I don't know how to dance."

"So, you think I dance like Hrithik Roshan?" replies Tarun and she laughs. "They will give us salsa lessons. By the way, feel free to invite Ritu, in case you feel more comfortable in her presence."

Every inch of her being wants to go out with Tarun. But she is worried how she will manage the dancing bit. She imagines herself falling down in the middle of pro salsa dancers and being surrounded with people who are laughing at her.

"Please!" pleads Tarun after a long silence, and she feels her struggle collapse.

I don't think I want to say no! In fact, I really want to go with him. He makes me feel so special.

"Yes, definitely. I will go with you," she finally replies, feeling less confident than she is trying to portray.

"Woohoo!" Tarun jumps up and does a victory dance.

Neha lets out a sigh and Tarun can almost feel her smiling through the phone.

Neha disconnects the call and her moment of weakness rises up again. "Shit! I hope I am able to get through this. I really want to."

> "*I owe it to myself to be more kind to me.*
>
> *Everyday, I am constantly reminded to accept the present and all it has to offer. After all, our present is an opportunity to begin afresh.*
>
> *No matter how much I try to let go, the best way is to take this new opportunity and try something different. After all, life is a collection of experiences, and to get rid of old ones, you need to make new ones.*"

13

Neha opens her apartment door and gets in. She takes a deep breath as she remembers her plan of going out with Tarun. *I just hope Ritu agrees to go with me.* She thinks as she walks to her room.

When she opens the door to Ritu's room, she finds Ritu clicking selfies.

"I wonder how many selfies does she click in a day," Neha mutters with a grin on her face.

Ritu looks at Neha's reflection in the mirror and spins around to look at her. "Now don't get started about my selfies!" she says, tossing down her mobile phone.

Ritu glances at Neha and smiles. "Tell me, what's going on?"

Neha stands there, not saying a word.

"I know you want to tell me something, so spill the beans!"

"Tarun asked me out for a salsa dance night at the Footloose discotheque tonight."

Ritu grabs Neha's arms and revolves her around. "This is awesome! You are going out with Tarun! I am so happy."

"I want you to come with me. Please!"

"Can I bring Gaurav?"

"No you cannot! Only you can come and you have to sit in between us." She giggles. "Of course you can bring him, how else do you plan to do salsa alone?

"Awesome, then I am in." She walks up and hugs Neha. "I am so glad. There were days I had to beg you to go out and today you are asking me to come out. You have come a long way, Neha. And I am so proud of you." She kisses her lightly on the cheek. "Okay, let me call Gaurav and fix the plan."

Neha gets up and starts to reach for her clothes to get dressed.

Ritu grabs her hand and pulls her back "What are you planning to wear?"

Neha smiles weakly and bites her lower lip. "I am not going to wear a..."

"Yes that's my condition. I will only go if you wear a dress."

Neha looks at her, confused. "But..."

"No buts, please. Last time I didn't force you, but this time, it's different. You can't be wearing a sweatshirt and jeans to a salsa night!"

"Then, I am not going." Neha shakes her head.

"Neha!"

"Why are we even discussing this? You know how I feel about all this. I don't feel comfortable when people stare at my body."

"Stop worrying about what other people think. Dress up for yourself; dress up for Tarun!"

"Ritu," Neha says with clenched teeth, "the last time I wore a skirt, I got raped. And I am not able to forget that."

"Neha, sweetheart! You are doing so good. Maybe, this is the last step to get you out of your own cage. Tarun is trying to help you, whether you realize it or not." She looks into Neha's eyes. "You should try it. You will look beautiful. And when you are with Tarun and us, you will feel beautiful too. What say?"

"Don't play guilt games on me! You know I won't be able to defend this logic." She walks back and forth in the room, trying to settle her heart rate down.

"But what I am saying is correct, isn't it?" asks Ritu.

Neha pulls back with a pout. "You know what, I don't even have a dress," Neha counters.

Ritu wraps Neha up in her arms. "Don't worry about that! We are going shopping," exclaims Ritu victoriously, and she runs to the shoe rack to wear her shoes.

"But don't forget, if I get a nervous breakdown, you will be held responsible."

"Babe, calm down! It's going to be good. You're gonna look stunning tonight. It's going to be perfect."

Tarun is just as worried as Neha is.

I have lost my mind. I should have considered before speaking up. I should have never listened to Gaurav for this salsa idea. Probably he wanted to go with Ritu and he pushed me into asking Neha. I don't even know how to dance. Maybe I can call at the last minute and pretend to be ill? But then, I don't have much time, I need to do it now.

"What the hell are you thinking?" Gaurav asks glancing down at him.

"If my hand wasn't broken, I would have punched you in the nose. That's what I am thinking." Gaurav looks over at him as his mouth drops open. "I should have never listened to your stupid idea of a salsa night!"

"You should be thanking me, and you are getting mad at me?" Gaurav gives him a confused look. "What? Why?"

"I don't know how to dance! I have a broken hand and I have never been out with a girl. I don't know if I will be able to manage it."

Gaurav stands there, just staring at him. "Wow! Somehow, you think someone can understand everything but then you just rattled off." He sits back down. "Okay, so let me get this straight. Neha has agreed to go out with you. She doesn't care how good a dancer you are. She just wants to spend time with you because she likes that. That's all that you should remember."

"Maybe, you are right."

Just then, Gaurav's cell phone rings.

"Hi baby, what's up?" Gaurav's face lights up on hearing Ritu's voice.

"I want to talk to Tarun," she says.

"Maybe this isn't the best time," Gaurav says.

"Just give the phone to him!" she says.

Gaurav hands over the phone to Tarun as he looks blankly at him.

"Hello Tarun!" she says, her voice as cheerful as can be. "Just make sure you dress up in your best possible formals and not a torn jeans and t-shirt, else I will kill you. Hope that is clear?"

"What?" Tarun is shell shocked. "But why?"

He had heard from Gaurav that Ritu was a bit dominating, but this was way too much.

"Just do as I say or you are dead. I will push you down the valley." She says this so coolly, as if she is discussing what to order in a restaurant. Then, she disconnects the phone just as abruptly.

My friend wants to kick my ass; his girlfriend wants to push me down the valley; I am going to a salsa night with Neha and

I don't know how to dance; and now I have to get dressed too. I wish I could kill Gaurav right now.

The guy standing at the bar laughs as he sees Tarun walk in. "Have you come to the wrong wedding?"

"Shut the fuck up!" Tarun hisses.

Here, he is at the Footloose discotheque in a black blazer, shirt and trousers, but not many people around him are that formally dressed. He feels that people are staring at him and gets very conscious.

"Look who's here!" says Ritu from somewhere behind, chirpy and loud as always.

Tarun smiles back at her but Gaurav is too stunned to give any expression on his face.

Ritu feels the heat of Gaurav's eyes burn a trail across her body. Even encased in the black dress that fell in soft folds just above her knees, she feels a bit exposed. When Gaurav's gaze lingers a little too long on the modest neckline that shows just a hint of cleavage, Ritu feels a quiver down her spine. Her shoulders are bare, the dress holding her back with thin straps, and she feels very warm as Gaurav's eyes move over them. Her breath gets caught in her throat as she sees the reaction his looks have caused. She feels as if she has just been caressed. *Oh, yes, this guy is definitely mine.*

Ritu hops and says in Tarun's ear, "Someone listened to me. Believe me, you won't be disappointed." She winks at him, and then swiftly grabs Gaurav and steps to the side.

Neha walks in. As she walks toward Tarun, he appreciates the elegantly understated black dress that is flattering her curves but is not flaunting them, unlike the revealing dresses chosen by many of the girls in the pub.

Her thick hair is wavy and bouncy which wants him to run his hand through it. He groans inwardly. *She looks like a princess.*

He looks at Neha's face – smooth and flawless, perfectly proportioned, and suggests just a hint of makeup. "You are looking absolutely gorgeous." He steps forward and kisses her on the cheek.

Neha feels a rush of warmth through her body at the simple words, adding to the flush that Tarun's direct gaze had just provoked.

Smiling, Neha says, "You are looking really handsome too." Tarun can feel his heart beating louder than the music in the pub.

Ritu and Gaurav bump into them and break the reverie. "Hey, lovebirds! We are heading to the bar," she says as she knots Gaurav's elbows and walks elegantly to the bar.

Neha can't help herself; she breaks into a deep laugh.

"God bless the bar tender tonight!" says Tarun.

Tarun looks around and then back at Neha. "I guess the four of us are the only ones who are dressed up?"

"Well, did Ritu threaten you too?"

"Yes, she did."

Neha tries to control her smile, though unsuccessfully. She chuckles and touches Tarun's hand. Shock waves runs up and down her spine as she feels the warmth of his hand.

Sliding the palm of her hand slowly down on his, she says, "I am glad I came here."

Neha is amazed at how much she is enjoying every second she is spending with Tarun. She can't remember a time when she had taken pleasure in the company of a guy.

Tarun draws a shaky breath. "I am glad too."

They walk towards the bar, hand in hand. "Would you like something to drink?"

"Yes, thank you."

Tarun moves his hand to call the bartender. Neha can still feel the warmth, even without the touch. Tarun continues with a taunt in his voice, "Since we are all dressed up, I suppose we should order something sophisticated to match our dress codes." He smirks at Ritu.

"Ya sure. You are right! Let's see. Gaurav and I will have Margaritas." Ritu says with a smile.

"Okay! Two Margaritas," Tarun repeats the same to the bartender and then turns around to Neha. "What would you like to drink?"

"Can you get anything made with strawberries?" asks Neha, and she turns and smiles lovingly at Tarun.

"Strawberry Daiquiris work for you?" the bartender says with a smirk. He is clearly showing off his talent of knowing more cocktails than they would have imagined, especially for a bartender in Shimla.

"As long as it has real strawberries and not syrup!" replies Neha.

The bartender flips some shakers through the air and makes their drinks swiftly. He looks more like a juggler in an act rather than a bartender. He walks back with their drinks neatly poured in cocktail glasses with a cute mini umbrella on each glass.

Tarun turns to Neha and raises his glass to offer a toast. He feels a tad unwell, but does not want to spoil the party.

"Cheers! For being able to try new things!"

"Cheers! For getting the courage to break out of our shells," Neha replies.

"To great friendship and fun times!" Ritu and Gaurav chime in, raising their glasses.

Due to the cocktail-induced courage, Tarun manages to hit the dance floor with Neha. He is so conscious of being overdressed that he feels everyone is just staring at him. He is anxious and uncomfortable as the dance trainer tries to show him what to do.

"So, the basic stance of the dance goes like this – you need to take her hand like this," he says, placing Neha's left hand in his as they face each other, "and then put your right hand on her shoulder."

She winks at Tarun and holds his hand tenderly as the dance trainer moves them into the correct positions, and then he starts to walk them through the steps.

"From the top – 5 6 7 8. Left foot forward," he speaks out, as they drag their feet clumsily on the dance floor. Tarun is staring down at Neha's heels the entire time and still somehow keeps stepping on her toes.

"That's good, you're fast learners," lies the trainer and he stops them to explain the next step.

"Now I will teach you how to spin your partner," he announces. Neha smiles and Tarun can't tell if she's anxious or eager.

"You need to lift your hand and..." He trails off as he sees the cast on Tarun's hand. "Oh god, your hand seems to be broken," he points out.

"Oh really, I didn't notice!" Tarun exclaims animatedly. "When did this happen?

Neha laughs at his dumb act, and he feels happy to have made her smile. The trainer rolls his eyes at him.

Eventually, Tarun follows Neha's steps rather than the trainer's voice, and that seems to click for him better.

"Enough of this! Now it's time for some fun," shouts Ritu as she glides next to them, along with Gaurav. They dance to the beats, following some rules, breaking others, but having fun. After all, that's what life is all about.

Tarun's eyes never leave Neha's as they roll on the dance floor. Neha is dancing and swaying to the music and seems to be having a good time.

Gaurav and Ritu are getting along pretty well in this dance. Gaurav reaches up and lifts her hand with his right hand and rolls her around into a spin. He winks at Tarun who takes that as his cue to mimic them.

"Are you holding up well?" Tarun asks. Neha turns her head to look at him and gives him a shy smile.

"Then, get ready to hold on really well!" Tarun grins as he propels her out for a swirl.

Neha giggles as she stoops under his arm and spins out away from him. Her dress billows up around her, flaunting her slender, exceptionally sexy legs. Tarun tries his best to look away from them, but is helplessly glued.

As the song turns slow, Neha spins again and pulls away. Tarun helps her complete the spin and she stumbles, but Tarun catches her right on time and holds her close. "Don't worry, I am there for you, sweetheart," he whispers in her ear.

Tarun can see Ritu watching them as he pulls Neha closer. Her only reply is to wrap her arms around Tarun's waist and lay her head on his chest. She fits perfectly in his arms.

Neha sighs deeply. *I am so happy in this moment, that I don't want it to end ever.*

Before they even realize it, the song is over and another slow one begins. Neha makes no move to pull away and it looks like it would take a small army to pull them away from each other. They smile, finding bliss in each other.

Neha adjusts her hold on Tarun and wraps her arm all the way around his waist.

Neha wonders how she got the courage to do so. *I don't even know how to express these feelings. Something tells me he's feeling it too.*

Tarun places a soft kiss on her forehead and she closes her eyes, enjoying the feel of him in her arms.

"You feel good in my arms," Tarun says. *I'm with the girl of my dreams and I've never been happier in my life.*

"We should dance more often," Neha kisses him on his cheeks.

She tips her head back and their eyes collide. There was no teasing or amusement there, only a hint of love that none of them was trying to hide. A stab of guilt sweeps over Tarun. He wants to tell her how he feels, but just cannot.

"I need to take a break," says Tarun as he is feeling really unwell.

He goes and sits on a chair, but even that doesn't make him feel any better. So he dizzily walks to the restroom, making it just in time. He throws up. Not once, but twice. There is some blood, just like the last time when he was at the Irish Bar. It leaves him exhausted and broken. He manages to walk back to the chair, trying to get a sip of water.

"Are you okay, Tarun?' Neha comes and sits down next to him, her cheeks flushed from the dancing.

"I feel a bit odd in my stomach. Maybe some food allergy or stomach infection. Maybe, the snacks weren't so good," Tarun lied.

"You want to go back?" she is concerned.

"No, no! I just need to sit down for a moment and rest." He manages to say while a new wave of giddiness sweeps over him.

Neha intertwines her fingers with his. "Is there anything I can do for you?"

He shakes his head, and she stays seated, tapping her foot to the music.

"Please go and dance! I want you to have a good time," Tarun says after a while.

"I am here to spend time with you. I don't care if we are dancing or just sitting together."

Tarun takes a deep breath. If she knew why he was feeling so unwell, she would leave everything and just sit beside him. He didn't want to be a sudden speed bump on her highway to recovering out of her dark past.

"Maybe, we can go out and get some fresh air?" Neha suggests and he complies.

He stands up with great difficulty, like an old man. She puts his arm over her shoulder and accompanies him outside.

"I think I should take you home," she looks at Tarun with concern in her eyes.

"I think that's a good idea." Tarun is relieved.

"

Try new things; make new goals.

What if I'm no good? What will people say? Get rid of such questions. The only way to take the first step towards happiness is to try new things. While recovering from a loss, I could only think about it all day. So I decided to try something new – maybe playing an instrument or some sort of exercise that would make me focus on a new challenge.

From a person who would never exercise, I have become a person who rides a bicycle 20 kms a day, five days a week. Just by changing my goal and outlook towards it, and taking small steps has helped me move ahead in life.

"

14

"I imagined this evening a little differently," said Tarun

"Why do you say so? I had a lot of fun and did things I have never done before." She rubbed his hands. "It's okay. I am still having a good time. Whenever I am with you, I have the best time of my life."

They walk along the Mall Road in silence, their hands still clasped, below the lights of the lamp posts.

By mutual consent, they stay in the shadows, keeping to the trees as they walk towards her apartment. Tarun is feeling much better now and doesn't want this night to end. She neither.

"I like being with you," she says softly. "Like this," she squeezes Tarun's hand. "I think it's romantic."

"What? Holding hands?"

"Yes. It has an intimacy of its own."

She stops, finding them next to a giant cedar tree, their shadows mixing with those of the trees around them.

She moves closer. She knows there is no use trying to prolong the inevitable.

Tarun can't seem to catch his breath, Neha's words stealing it away from him. She comes so close to pulling him into her, so close to kissing him right here. Tarun has been waiting for her to do just that. Neha bends her head, placing a light, delicate kiss on his lips, Tarun closes his eyes, loving Neha's gentleness.

And there is no rush this time, as they move into each other's arms, hands sliding on each other's cheeks, touching warm flesh, mouths meeting in a slow, tender kiss.

A tiny moan escapes as Tarun's hands slips around Neha's waist, pulling her closer. He can feel Neha tremble at his touch and his mouth opens, their kisses turning hungry as their bodies melt.

Neha breathes heavily, turning her head to expose more of her neck to Tarun's lips, loving the feel as they move against her skin. Her breath comes faster as she loses herself in Tarun's kisses. Yes, they should stop. But it is the furthest thing on her mind as her hand glides up his side, brushing her fingertips across his chest. She is so close to him she can feel the beats of his heart.

"I love kissing you," Tarun says, moving against Neha's lips. "Kissing you, touching you."

Neha's mouth moves across his skin, her breath whispering into his ear. "I've dreamed of kissing you many times. I can't believe how nervous I am."

"I'm guessing your dreams didn't include me up against a tree with a potential audience within few feet of us."

She smiles at his comment, but does not stop. She releases Tarun's hand and moves a step closer, her bare legs brushing against Tarun's trousers, her face, her mouth, only inches away from his. "It is so good to be with you. How? I can just get lost in your eyes, Tarun. Just being around you, like this, I feel things I haven't felt in so many years, it's simply amazing."

"I can't tell you how happy I feel with you." Tarun says.

Neha smiles back at him as they start walking down the hill toward Tarun's apartment. Tarun puts an arm around her waist, but instead of the uneasy terror she usually feels, she is calm and affectionate.

This is how I always want it to be. Neha thinks.

As they cross the long passage and reach his apartment, they enter a cosy, empty and silent living room since Gaurav has decided to stay with Ritu after the dance is over.

"So what did you like most today?" Tarun looks up in her eyes, his gaze finding her.

She smiles. "Mmmm.. let me see. The salsa dance, or the margarita or the dance trainer…" She stops and looks straight into the eyes. "Actually, I know the answer."

"Please enlighten me too." Tarun smiles as she spins and comes into his arms.

"The best part of the night was dancing with you," she says "I have never felt this comfortable with any guy, as I felt with you. And I am happy that you helped me come out of my shell by planning this evening."

His smile is so wide and happy that you'd think he had just received a big reward.

When Neha turns her head, Tarun is waiting, and their lips meet, softly, gently. Neha opens up under his lips, accepting him. Nervous panic flickers to life inside her head instantly, but the incredible warmth spreading through her body quickly smothers her terror and ignites a flaming desire in its place. *How much she wants this guy!* She reached blindly for him. They take what they both need, what they both want, up against the wall. Pent up desire releases a storm through them. They have been wanting to be close, and now they can't resist any further.

"This was the best part about the night for me," he mutters.

Disoriented and confused, Neha tries to look at him. She isn't sure if she is ready. But she has not had nearly enough of Tarun's sweet kisses. She is stunned by the desire she sees in Tarun's eyes, hoping that her own eyes reflect as much. She feels captivated by those eyes. She just can't look away.

She kisses him again to divert herself from the feeling, but all it does is make the feeling grow stronger inside her. But this time, there is no rush as they move into each other's arms, hands sliding on each other's back, mouths meeting in a slow, tender kiss.

"I love kissing you," Tarun says, moving against her lips. "Kissing you, touching you."

Neha's mouth moves across his skin, her breath whispering into his ear. "I've dreamed of this for so long, but I can't believe how nervous I am."

Tarun slides his hands up, cupping her face again. "Don't be nervous. I just want it to be normal. I want to be there for you, for better or worse."

She moves her hands, feeling Tarun's hard shoulder against her palms. "And god, I want my mouth back on yours," she says as she finds his lips again.

They continue to kiss. A strange feeling is taking over her senses, and she loves it. Truth be told, she had never given any man much of a chance.

Neha realizes that this is the furthest she has ever made it with him. The last time he came close to her, she had flipped out. But not this time.

Her mind frantically races back and forth, the kiss giving her internally the same chills that her outer body was experiencing. She wanted more.

She lies back on the sofa, and pulls Tarun on top of her. That makes Tarun nervous. *What if she reacts like she did in the skating rink when I fell on her? What if she starts crying and runs away?*

"Neha, I want to know if you are okay with this?" he asks apprehensively.

Neha smiles back warmly, attempting to conceal her nervous energy. She winds her hands into his short, thick, black hair and pulls him down to the couch. She gasps as Tarun's tongue parts her lips and begins a subtle dance. Tarun's hand caresses her side, each movement drawing her closer to him.

Neha's head spins in anticipation, but then he stops suddenly and looks doubtfully at her. "Are you okay?"

"Yes, I'm fine," Neha whispers breathlessly. "I want to continue, and I want it to be with you, Tarun."

"But promise me that you'll not run away. You will tell me if I am hurting you." He looks worried. "Because I don't want to lose you, Neha."

It was at this moment that Neha realizes how lucky she is. Even with all the problems she has, Tarun wants to be with her and is trying his best to ensure that she is comfortable.

She simply nods and pushes him onto the couch. "Maybe, I need to be on top to make sure I am in control and I don't get a panic attack."

She feels her body heating up as Tarun pulls her closer. The spark between them turns into roaring flames as he moves his body in sync with her.

Neha is worried that the demons from her past will get unleashed, but she continues to kiss him.

Tarun tries to cover the ugly, jagged scar that was a constant reminder of all his pain with his hand. She removes his hand and kisses his scar tenderly.

"Neha? As much as I want this, I don't want you to feel hurt in any way."

"Work with me sweetheart, so that I can get rid of my demons," she whispers in his ear. "I want you."

When her eyes meet his, he forgets all his warnings to stay away and leans in to kiss her again. The kiss is coaxing, slow and sultry. Neha tries to chant his name, but her voice is effectively muffled beneath his kiss and her moans. She responds instead by kissing him back, just as sweetly and seductively.

The tenderness he shows proves to be every bit as devastating as the heat generating from his body.

"Mmm..." she gestures weakly, arching her back as Tarun licks her neck. "Tarun, I want—" Hushed words of desire swirl within the confines of the apartment. Tarun utters soft, tortured moans as he moves his shivering hands on her quivering legs. His fingers skirt her calves, below the knees before disappearing beneath her skirt. Dheeraj triggers to life inside her head, leering at her as he lifts her skirt.

No way! This can't be happening. Dheeraj isn't doing this to me. Not tonight – not after how hard I've tried to break the chains! My fiery craving for Tarun is stronger than my fears tonight.

She tries hard to focus in the moment, where she has Tarun. The terrifying image of Dheeraj disappears as quickly as it emerged.

As his hands move on her legs, he feels entrapped in his desire to have her and the fear of not having her. Neha tries to unfasten the buttons along his formal shirt. Her hands ache to caress his chest. She manages to unbutton and move her hand inside his shirt and Tarun arches back at her sudden touch. His touch beneath her skirt grows bolder. His sensuous lips feast on her lips while his fingers try to search and discover the treasure.

They spend the next few hours feeling each other, exploring each other. Tarun knows he is opening his heart for Neha. Whoever he has earlier cared for, has either left him or died. He has been hurt too badly in the past and he doesn't want to go through that again. Ever.

Neha feels grateful about how sensitive Tarun has been. She knows that if she had insisted on stopping, Tarun would have agreed without hesitation, and she would have been miserable in the morning. But that wasn't what she needs. Tarun was there for her, that's what her heart and body said. The attraction between them was real, that was all there was. All there ever could be.

> "*Loving and listening are the two best things you can do for your partner who is trying to recover from a past tragedy or a broken heart. Many times, there isn't much you can do to take the pain away. But you can be there – even if it's just to hold each other.*"

15

Tarun has hardly woken up peacefully ever. This morning, however, Tarun is feeling really happy. He remembers the last night.

The soothing, heavy spray of water sleeked and beaded across his frame as he stand beneath the shower head that morning. He kept thinking about last night. He'd gone to bed, thinking about Neha and woken up with her thoughts. Being with her again is all that he wanted.

He shut off the water and dried off, but his thoughts remained about Neha as he dresses up and heads out of the door.

Outside, the sun shone weakly, showering warm light. He felt great standing there, taking in the view of the horizon as he waited for the bus.

Neha gazes at the red numbers on her bedside clock. "Sat 10:30 A.M." She cannot believe she has slept past the alarm time. She usually wakes up before the alarm rings, but today is different. She has woken up from a peaceful sleep after a long time. She had dreams instead of nightmares. Her dreams were filled with Tarun and she couldn't get him out of his mind.

She manages to get up ,wash her face and brush her teeth. Then, she heads to the kitchen to fix breakfast, but the thought of Tarun, lying next to her on the couch keeps coming back to her. Neha keeps smiling as she adds peppers and onions to her omelette mixture. If only, she could go back to last night.

It's Saturday. Neha has lots to do. She has to remember to send applications for the placement week, but right now, the only thing that matters to her is thinking about Tarun.

Just as she is lost in his thoughts, her mobile rings.

She jumps up in joy and swipes the answer button. "Hey!"

"Hi Neha…"

Tarun's voice is affectionate and soft, and somehow nothing else matters when she hears him say her name.

"What's going on?" Tarun asks.

"Umm… nothing much. I was just making breakfast. What about you?"

"Well, I actually just woke up after the first peaceful sleep of my life. And then, got ready and came to the market to get some notes photocopied. But truly speaking, I don't feel like doing anything but spending time with you."

Neha smiles. "I too woke up pretty late today. I guess we both had a pretty long night yesterday."

"Actually, I'll be honest. You were the girl in my dreams all through last night. I kept dreaming about you all night and woke up missing you next to me."

"That's so sweet of you. I missed you too, Tarun."

"I was just calling to check if we can meet tonight," he asks Neha, his voice stiff and worried. "Maybe, we can watch a movie?"

"Sure, that would be great."

"Awesome! So, see you in the evening?" Tarun jumps up with joy.

"See you tonight!" she says, happily before hanging up.

"So, who are you seeing tonight, girl?" Ritu comes, yawning into the apartment, after a rendezvous with Gaurav and seems really hung over.

"I have made an omelette for you too and it's lying next to the stove," she avoids Ritu's question.

"Thanks, you are a sweetheart. I am so lucky to have you. But that doesn't let you off the hook," Ritu smirks.

"Means?"

"Means that you still got to tell me about what happened last night and who are you going out with," Ritu answers.

"Oh, last night was awesome," Neha blushes as she pours herself a cup of tea. "I wish I had words to describe it. It was like nothing I have felt ever before."

"Hmm…" Ritu picks up her plate before joining her at the table.

"What about your night, madam?"asks Neha.

She smiles slyly at Neha before answering. "You really want to know the details of what happened in the bedroom?"

"Actually no," Neha stutters, shaking her head. "I think I can live without those details!"

She knows that Ritu will give here exact details of what happened with Gaurav, and the next time she sees Gaurav, she will find it very awkward to face him.

"I thought so," she replies and winks at Neha.

Ritu finds the omelette very tasty, but the tea is dark and extra strong. Just as Neha likes to have it, with almost no milk and no sugar.

"I am so glad you came out dancing," Ritu says, "and that too, all groomed up, in a skirt."

Neha has no clue how to respond to this, so she munches at her food and rolls her eyes. "I don't know how to explain the feeling. I felt transported to a place where I was surrounded by love, warmth and happiness. Something that I have never felt before."

Ritu feels happy for Neha. She realizes that Neha is deeply in love with Tarun and so is he. She herself, is feeling really happy as she has found her love, Gaurav and it feels great to have someone by your side, for ever.

"What are those papers in your hand?" asks Neha.

Well, a company is coming to college for placement, SATA Consulting Services!" she says cheerfully, hugging Neha with her other hand. "I have been invited for an interview!"

"This is so amazing!" Neha jumps up in her seat. "I knew it, you had to get this!"

"They usually only take two to three students from our college and they have shortlisted me!" she chirps enthusiastically.

"Is it the best day of our life, or what?" Neha says.

"What about you? Any interviews lined up?" Ritu asks, and Neha shakes her head. The placement week starts just in fifteen days, and she feels as if time has just flown away.

"Don't you worry. I am sure you will do great," she tells Neha.

"You know how scared I was in the last interview. I have been so introvert that it's very hard to face the real world."

"Hmm."

"Plus, you know I don't want to go back to my home. I want a job elsewhere."

"I am sure you will crack it," Ritu answers with an assuring smile.

"I hope so too." Neha replies rolling her eyes.

"And, are you going to tell me more about last night or no?"

"I need to first understand what's going on," Neha replies softly. "My heart is saying something, but my brain is saying something else, and my past is pulling me back. After what happened last night, I should be running into Tarun's arms, hugging him, kissing him, telling him how special he is to me. But deep inside, I'm also a bit scared. I lost control of myself last night, and as wonderful as it felt, it was scary to feel myself do things I'd never thought I'd do."

"Welcome to the world of love, darling," Ritu says, reaching out and hugging Neha. "This is how you feel when you are in love."

"Really?"

"Maybe at a later stage, it may make more sense. Putting your trust in someone definitely gives you all the love, but it also comes with a sense of insecurity till you are not sure of the person."

Neha's shoulders droop. "I am going around with someone for the first time in my life, I am an emotional wreck. And even my best friend knows nothing about romance! God, help me!"

"Go ahead and try it for yourself!" Ritu says, "but please be careful." She fixes her dark eyes on Neha.

"Why do you keep saying that?" Neha props her fist beneath her chin and studies her best friend for a long while

"Listen, sweetie. One does stupid things in love. All I am saying is that you both need to be sure of your feelings."

> "*Don't hold back. When you feel love, go all in. We've most likely all been hurt before, and I'm not saying we should disregard those situations. All I am saying is that don't let past hurts prevent you from making new relationships or falling in love. Don't be afraid to love deeply. It can be scary to depend on anyone. Be open. Be brave.*"

16

It's not that cold outside at six o'clock when Tarun leaves his apartment and starts off for the short walk to Neha's place for his movie date. It's a pleasant change from the usual super cold Shimla winter. It will be summer soon, anyway.

Tarun suddenly gets nervous at the thought that his parents would force him to come home during summer break again. His mother has been constantly messaging him since a few days, requesting him to come home. He has been purposely ignoring the messages.

He tries to lock down the thoughts in some closet in the farthest corner of his mind as he reaches Neha's apartment. He is really looking forward to their movie date tonight and does not want his dominating father to ruin his evening by empowering his mind.

He rings the doorbell and hears Neha shout at the top of her voice. "I'll get it." He hears her footsteps followed by hushed voices of a few people. She swings open the door and smiles, shyly at him.

"There is a slight issue," she says.

"Well, that wasn't the kind of greeting I was expecting," he replies with a smile.

"I am sorry. Actually the girls next door have a broken television so they checked with Ritu and came over," she explains, pointing at the living room couches filled with four girls, Bacardi Breezer bottles and chips-packets on the centre table.

"Is it possible that we go to your apartment instead?" asks Neha.

"I wish we could." Tarun sighs, looking up at the sky, cursing his luck.

"Why not?"

"Your dear friend Ritu and my lovable friend Gaurav have occupied the living room for their movie date," Tarun says.

"Oh no!" Neha replies stamping her foot on the ground.

"I think we can cancel the movie plan and maybe go for a walk instead? And have our movie date next Saturday? " asks Tarun, trying to make the best of whatever time he has with Neha.

"If you are cool with it, then maybe we can watch it in my room, on a laptop?" Neha suggests. "We may not have a big television, but we will still have us."

"Awesome, sounds like a plan!" Tarun replies elatedly, as he sees Neha's smile widening every second.

As Tarun takes the first step towards her room, he remembers Ritu's threats from a few hours ago. He slowly follows her, trying not to look at her. Neha is wearing a lemon-coloured woollen dress with black slacks and the way the dress is hugging her is making him go crazy.

The girls in the living room let out hushed giggles as they cross the room. They reach the far end and her room is on the left. As Tarun enters inside, he is awestruck, looking at the immaculate room – every book in its right place, every loose paper put away. Basically, everything in perfect order.

She comes and sits close to him, and his heart thumps out of his chest as their legs touch. Her shoulder brushes against his, and he takes a deep breath to cool himself down.

Neha switches on her laptop and clicks on the Netflix app. She scrolls down for Tarun so that he can select a movie of his choice, but his eyes remain glued to her.

"What genre of movie do you want to watch – action, romance?" she asks.

"Whatever you want."

"No, but you need to give me some idea of what you like?"

She looks up at him and he gets lost in her gorgeous eyes for a long time before finally snapping out of his dream and replying. "I am okay with whatever you select. The fact is that I am getting to spend time with you means the world to me."

She smiles at his romantic comment. "But still, help me pick one," she asks again, elbowing him to focus on the screen.

"Neha, I will be okay with any movie you chose, I promise," he replies, gently putting his arm around her shoulder. She leans into him, and he sighs contentedly as he feels the warmth of her body against his.

"You're not just saying that to make me feel good?"

"It doesn't matter if we watch a good movie or a bad movie or no movie at all," he says affectionately, and then he kisses her on her forehead. "I just want to spend time with you."

Her eyes beam up at his meaningful words and he can feel the unseen wall of apprehension between them fall to pieces.

"Then, let's not watch a movie!" she says softly. "What if we just spend the night talking to each other? Maybe, we can make some snacks and grab a drink?"

"Did you just read my mind?" Tarun smirks as his lips notch up a little. She smiles back and they walk to the kitchen.

Neha guides him to different cabinets and he pours the chips and crackers in bowls while she starts searching for something inside the cabinets.

"Where did it go?" she mumbles with her face, fully inside the cabinet.

He hears the sound of some utensils banging with each other.

"Yess! Found it!" She appears from the kitchen shelf with her hair now messy, a victorious smile on her face and a bottle of Old Monk rum clutched in her hand.

"Let's make this winter a bit warmer tonight," she says, pouring a shot into each of their glasses, winking at him." Now don't start judging me, okay! Sometimes when Ritu is feeling really cold, she drinks this with hot water."

"Don't you think that drink is supposed to be brandy and not rum?" Tarun asks.

"Maybe, but this is what Ritu thought was the better option considering the cold climate of Shimla."

"I have full confidence in Ritu's choice." He grinned. "After all, she chose you as her best friend."

She scoots back to the doorway of her room and then, waves to him, eagerly from there.

I look at the rum in my hand, and then, at her beaming innocent face. My life has been a collection of worsts, but this is the first time I feel I have found the best – the best girlfriend in the whole universe.

> "*Treasure your love.*
>
> *Once you find someone who makes you feel any of these three things, make sure you treasure them for life: one, time spent doesn't feel better because of a large screen television but because of their company. Two, home is not really a place, but a feeling. And three, heartbeats are not just heard, but can be felt and shared in precious moments.*"

17

Neha dips the crackers in the rum-and-coke-filled glass and munches them. "Have you tried the crackers like this?" she says. "Oh, they taste yummy."

"I have never heard or seen anyone dip a cracker in a drink. You are the first," he says smiling at her as he takes the first sip.

"I am happy to be your first," she says with a sly smile.

Tarun smiles back and dips a bunch of potato chips in her drink. Then, he teases her by sticking out his tongue and she laughs out loud.

"So, we've got rum and plenty of chips and crackers," Tarun says, lying back against the cushions. "Now, all we need is to spice it up a bit."

"Umm, let me see. How do we do that ?" She chews a potato chip slowly, thinking about what to do next. "I know what we can do!"

"And what would that be? Dipping the rest of the food in the kitchen in rum?"

"No no, I have a better idea. We can play truth or dare?"

"You need more people to play that! It can't be just you versus me. Can it be?" Tarun argues.

"Oh, come on! Don't chicken out. Actually it's the best with two people playing it!"

"Really? How is that?" he continues to grumble.

"Two reasons. First, it's just you and me and that makes it special. And second, I trust you and I can share my secrets," she says, in a serious tone.

Tarun understands what she means. They definitely needed to talk and open up to each other. "Then, it's better to play truth and forget the dare part," he says.

"I might dare you for something fun," Neha teases. "Plus, there's alcohol in our body, so we can hold it responsible for whatever dumb thing we do."

"That's a good idea!" he humours her by acting like an alcoholic.

"What are we waiting for? Let's play! Truth or dare?" Tarun asks, pointing a cracker at her.

"Truth."

"Uh, actually, I need a minute," Tarun stutters. "I am not yet sure of what to ask."

She smiles and has a sip of her drink.

"Tell me an embarrassing moment of yours."

"Of all the things, this is what you ask?" she grumbles, and Tarun smirks back with raising his eyebrows.

She rests back, lying close to him on the cushions.

Tarun tries really hard not to stare at her dress which is easing out at her shoulders.

"When I was a kid, one day I was feeling really sick. I told this friend of mine, sitting next to me that I wanted to go home as I wasn't feeling well. She kept scaring me that the teacher would be really angry. But finally, when the teacher saw me, making a really bad face, she asked me what was wrong and if I needed any help.

"Before I could say anything, I actually vomited on my friend, sitting next to me."

"That's terrible!" he says, even though he's laughing really hard.

"No, it was worse," Neha continues. "You should have seen her face." That makes him laugh even harder.

"And she was no more my friend from that day."

Tarun continues laughing.

"Your turn now. Truth or dare?"

"Dare!" replies Tarun

Neha scrunches her nose, but then, there appears a devilish sparkle in her eyes. "I dare you to reply my question truthfully."

"Hello, that's not done. You are cheating!"

"It's either my way or the highway, you can choose," she says.

"Okay, sure. Then let's call this game truth and truth!"

"You are a very good boy," she smiles. "Who's the first girl you ever kissed?"

"You're the only girl for me, Neha," Tarun comes close and whispers in her ear.

"You are the only one for me too," she replies.

She is smiling now and kisses him on the cheek. Then, she slowly turns around to meet her lips. He kisses her carefully, like she might be this fragile thing that needs to be handled with caution. Her lips felt exquisitely soft as they brushed over his. It was a surprisingly tender kiss, less an act of passion and more of an offer of comfort.

"Your turn again. Truth or dare?" she asks.

"Give me a real dare, this time!" Tarun calls out, smiling mischievously.

Neha takes another sip of her drink and then whispers, "I dare you to kiss me as if your life depended on it."

He moves forward and holds the back of her neck tenderly, and draws his head down until he reaches her mouth. He can feel the cool silk of her hair against his fingers, impossibly soft. Opening his lips, he deepens the kiss, drinking in her taste, savoring the sweet comfort she offered.

Neha responds with a tiny moan, a whimper of breath against his mouth. She leans into him, her warm body pressed against his. Her long legs move restlessly, brushing his thighs.

It was slow, lazy, a thorough exploration of her mouth, as exquisitely tempting as it can be. He can feel the same impatience as her, but he hid it well, taking his time with the slow mating of mouths, teasing, stroking, lip-to-lip.

The kiss spun on, lazy and drugging. The taste of him is intoxicating – a hint of rum, a trace of chocolate, and above all, that dazzling masculinity.

He lingers on her lower lip and then draws back enough to smile into her eyes. The kiss has painted her cheeks rosy, made her dark eyes sparkle. A smile overtakes her features.

They both pause, neither of them knowing exactly how the air suddenly became so thick and heavy. He notices his hand has stopped touching her arm. Her fingers stopped running along his cheek. He holds his breath. She can hear his heart through his shirt, feel its beat accelerating.

"It's your turn now," Tarun murmurs. "Truth or…"

Before he can finish, Neha has pushed him back and is on top of him.

Neha runs her hand through his warm hair. He lifts his head and looks at her, his dark eyes holding the edge of desire that she is holding too. She kisses him again, their lips swollen, Neha nipping at him. Her scent is intoxicating him. Tarun makes a low, hungry sound in his throat and drags her up against his chest, his mouth slanting over hers. He eases her lips apart and slides her tongue with his. The taste of him fills her mouth, the scent of him teases her nose, and the hard, warm press of his body against hers, doing things to her she can barely believe are possible.

His lips feel electrified from her mouth, and his body was tight, anticipatory. He wants her and craves for the scent of her skin. Now that he has had her taste, the need for more is nearly overwhelming. It made his hands curl involuntarily at the thought of touching her silky bare body. He forcibly cages his desires as he doesn't want to hurt her.

The first kiss had been tame and tentative. This one contains wild desire. He runs his fingers through her hair, pulling her head back, moving to kiss her throat. She arches against him, the wild kiss arousing her like crazy.

He tries to stop, but she holds his hand firmly, her moans, hot and possessive.

"Neha," he breathes out, breaking the kiss. He presses her forehead to his chin and lets out a long, slow breath. "I think we should stop. As much as I am loving this—"

"No, don't stop!"

He can't control any further; she's too tempting. Before he can realize what he is doing, he grabs her by her soft round hips and rolls her over so that he is on top, looking down at her, and he kisses her passionately, pouring out his desire.

Tarun slants his mouth more firmly across her lips and plunges his tongue into her mouth as if to consume her. Sweet pleasure fills her, driving the chill from her bones and filling them with warm love.

He pulls her lower lip between his teeth, rasping it gently with his teeth, and her body quivers. With her eyes still firmly shut, Neha grabs his hand and pulls it to her knees. He knows what she wants but he is apprehensive. Neha doesn't stop and starts dragging her dress up with his hand.

"I want you more, Tarun," she pleads, biting her lower lip.

He wants her too, but doesn't want to hurt her. He listens to her wishes and moves his fingers slowly from her hips to her flat stomach, and then over her bra. He wants her, but the last fiasco keeps popping up in his mind. He just wants to be sure not to hurt her feelings.

"Neha? Are you okay with…?"

She stops his words with her mouth. Breaking the kiss, she whispers, "I want you to put your hands on me."

Using the pressure of her hand, he pulls up her dress and over her shoulders. She feels that there is something incredibly erotic about having him slowly undress her. The deliberate revealing of warm, bare flesh; the leisurely sliding of skin against skin.

Tarun's heart races madly as Neha releases his hand. His body responds to her craving. She presses back against him as his fingers reach under her bra and she snaps it out for him. He rasps the edge of his teeth along her skin, raising goose bumps and making her nipples go hard, then slides his tongue along her skin, heading toward her breasts.

"Neha…"

"I need you, Tarun!" Her eyes widen with desire as she pushes his hands lower towards her waist.

Tarun holds his hands at her waist and does not go further down.

"I want to do this, and I want to do it with you," she begs.

Then, he moves his hand slowly under her panties, moving his fingers slowly. He presses his finger against her, slowly increasing the pace. He is overwhelmed with feelings he never imagined existed. Now, he feels filled with the love he'd always needed from her, but thought he'd never be able to get.

Her head falls back into the pillows with a moan, and her spine arches as he presses further, filling her completely.

"More," she begs, her voice stuttering in between short breaths as she grinds her hips against him. She cries out as he follows her wishes and presses his fingers harder, leading her to a climax.

Instead of pleasure, the climax brings back sad memories. Despite trying so hard not to, Neha goes into a spiral of thoughts down the rabbit hole. *My heart races dangerously. My skin burns. My chest tightens. My lungs seem to go rigid. My fingers and toes itch. Things begin to go out of focus, then back in, and out again. Like looking through a kaleidoscope, it makes me dizzy. The room, the way it's spinning, the way the world ceases to make any sense at all. I hear this buzzing in the background, like static. Static pulsing through brain waves, electric currents floating around in this strange place, making the air feel nervous, activated somehow.*

"Back away from me!" Her voice sounds surprisingly panicked. It seems that something she has been holding in, all tightly sealed, has now bubbled up from her depths, bringing with it a swell of anger.

He quickly moves his hand out and hugs her tightly.

"Please, let me go, I beg you," she says, losing her voice to tears. The words come out through her teeth, and she's unable to stop the tears, like it hurts her to have to say it.

"It's me, Tarun," he assures her, still holding her close. "Your Tarun. You are safe with me."

Tarun lays by her side, close to her and he looks like he doesn't know what to do. She certainly doesn't know how to manage this either, so she moves forward and puts her arms around him. He hugs her back. They stay like that for a long time, not saying anything. Tarun feels like they could stay like this forever and it would still never be long enough.

"Why were you crying?" he finally asks.

"I can't say," Neha tries to breathe.

"Was it because of me?"

"No, it has nothing to do with you." She feels him exhale, next to her. "I'm sorry about all that, by the way."

"I'm sorry too." *I shouldn't have pushed her so far. I wish I could go back in time and fix whatever happened with her.*

They breathe against each other, and with every breath she exhales, she feels like she is getting lighter, like the residue from all those old, stagnant emotions is working its way out of her.

She starts drawing these invisible lines on his forearm. She mutters something indecipherable, and then, "One more round of truth or dare, please," she volunteers.

"Okay, truth or dare?" Tarun asks her.

"Truth."

"Is there something in your past which haunts you even today?" Tarun asks, and he prepares himself for the answer.

She nods and covers her eyes with her hands, because they're crying. These are tears of atrocity, of regret and not being able to do anything about any of it.

"I was raped when I was thirteen." Her voice breaks up as she tries not to cry. "By my brother's best friend," she murmurs, watching his eyes double in size.

"What?" he asks, seemingly shocked by her admission. She pinches her eyes closed, and searches to find the words to explain.

As soon as she opens her mouth to speak, he grabs her face in his hands. "I am so sorry."

"What?" she asks, pulling back.

His grip around her face tightens as he pulls her close to him again. "I'm sorry that it happened. No one should have to go through that." And that's all it takes before she is sobbing in his arms. "It's okay. I've got you now."

"I should never have gone to my brother's apartment," she cries, gripping Tarun's t-shirt, which is now soaked in her tears.

He grips her arms and pulls her to look at him. "It's not your fault. Do you hear me? None of this is your fault."

The air feels different – her tears, hugging Tarun tightly, the world, everything feels different. It all starts making sense to Tarun.

"I really want to experience love. And I am so glad that I found you. But every time, I come close to being so intimate, my past just blows up on me," she manages to say in between sobs. "It's a constant battle between my heart wanting to do it and the mind reminding me what happened to me."

All Tarun can do is hold her tight. "I am sorry Neha, and I wish I could undo it."

"I am the one who should be sorry," she argues, gulping in her tears. "Don't you get frustrated when I blow up and act like a maniac?"

Does she really believe that she's a burden to me? Meeting her is the best thing ever to happen to me! Tarun wonders. "You have accepted me despite my issues," Tarun says. "Then, what makes you think I would get frustrated and not stand by you when you need me?"

"Tarun, I can't control when the past comes back roaring into my mind," she mumbles, almost as if she's confessing a hideous crime. "Why do you want to waste your time with me? You are not messed up like me. You deserve someone better than me. At least, someone who is normal and can accept your love and reciprocate the feelings.

"I am as messed up as anyone can be," Tarun says, with conviction. "If I say that I don't deserve you because my family is all broken up with an alcoholic father who almost killed my childhood love and my only friend, then would you agree? Even today, I live in fear of my father and the guilt of not being able to stand up for my childhood friend!"

"But you are more important than all this. I don't care about your past. All I care about is that I have you in my life by my side Tarun!" she says solemnly.

"Exactly my point! You are more important to me than anyone in this world. I am not worried about your flashbacks, Neha. You have a pure heart and that's what I want you to remember. If you stay strong, you can walk past your dark past and have a great present where you are with me."

She smiles brightly at Tarun and hugs him warmly. For several minutes, they lie there together. Tarun is caressing her cheeks and comforting her as much as he can. That's when her eyes fall upon the tattoo on the inside of his arm and she can't stop her fingers from running over it.

"That's the date Aditi went away from my life. I put it there as a reminder," he says, looking down at her fingers.

"You'll never forget. She's right here," Neha whispers, resting her hand on his chest.

"Thank you for trusting me with your secret. I'm sorry about what happened. If I could go back and change it, I would," he says, running his fingers along her collarbone.

"The thing about past is that it can't be rewritten. Somehow, I have to learn to deal with it and you have to forgive yourself for what happened to Aditi."

"Sometimes it feels like I'm being punished for what happened that night," Tarun says softly, just a few inches from her lips.

"What do you mean?" she asks, pulling her head back to look into his eyes.

"I don't know. I guess everything bad that happens seems like god's way of paying me back." He pauses, moving his fingers up to caress her cheek. "But since I've met you, it feels like I've been given a second chance. It feels like I am living after a long time. And I owe this regret-free life to you."

"And I owe my happiness to you," Neha whispers, pressing her lips to his. "You've opened my eyes to so many things that I wouldn't let myself see before."

"I don't know what I did to deserve moments like these," he says, brushing a few strands of hair back from her forehead.

Neha understands his pain because she would be a mess if something ever happened to someone close to her. But he has to let go of the guilt that he's holding on to. He can't change what happened, no one can. She also realizes she is being a hypocrite because she has spent the last so many years holding on to a past she can't change.

"You deserve a lifetime of moments like these," Neha says, kissing him again. He reaches behind her head to deepen the kiss, paying attention to her lips first, and then pressing his tongue into her mouth. Her heart flutters when he slides his hand under her shirt to massage her lower back. She moans as he slows the kiss and pulls her lower lip between his teeth.

When she looks into his eyes again, she sees love mixed with concern. "If I ever push you too far and you want to stop, all you have to do is tell me. I'm not the type of guy who takes things from a girl that she doesn't want to give. I'm not him," he says, nuzzling his nose with hers. "I need you to remember that you always have control. Always."

> "*Just because your partner doesn't immediately tell you her thoughts doesn't mean he/she isn't willing to share. While opening up their secrets might help some people process their emotions, other people need time to sort out their feelings. Even if it takes a couple of days for your partner to open up, give them that space. The day that emotional discussion happens, it will develop a deep level of trust in your relationship.*"

18

Neha is facing the other way when she wakes up. Tarun is hugging her, still. With his body joined with hers like this, she gets the feeling that his arms are holding her broken pieces together.

She feels him press his face into her hair and kiss her in his sleep and closes her eyes. *I want to freeze this moment, want to stay just like this, and never have to do or think or feel or be anything else at all.*

She turns around to face him, just in time to hear him whisper, "I love you."

"I love you, too," she echoes.

"Did you get some sleep?" he asks softly.

She nods in response and cuddles up closer to him. "And you?"

"Yes, I got some sleep too," he whispers.

Why does everything suddenly feel different? Lighter? Why do I feel like, for once in my life, I might really have some control over what happens next.

Tarun pulls her up against his chest and slants his lips over hers. His tongue slips within her mouth and warms her up, making her forget her insecurities, making her forget all the other painful incidents of her past.

When they break the kiss, she draws a trembling breath. A look of happiness envelopes her face. "Oh, Tarun!" She reaches up and cups his cheeks. "I am scared this is all a dream and it would vanish when you leave. I will have nothing left in my life."

"I have everything because I have you. And I am not going anywhere."

"Even if I keep behaving crazily?"

"We'll figure it out." She smiles back, warmly. "I am here for you. But I am afraid that you won't be able to stand my broken family. I don't want them to cause you any pain."

"If you are with me, I am ready to face the world," she says confidently, and kisses him on the cheek.

"Tarun... even I want...," Neha hesitates, falling short of words. She is too self-conscious to say what she wants.

"You don't have to think twice, Neha. Tell me," he assures her.

"I want to explore you, too," Neha lies down on his chest before talking again. "May I?"

"But I have more scars than you can imagine."

"I don't care." Her fingers start unbuttoning his shirt. She dusts her lips across his bare chest, tasting his skin with the tip of her tongue and feeling his muscles tremble as she pushes his shirt up and over his head. The touch of her hands makes him shiver, makes him groan.

She runs her palms over his chest, hardly able to believe that all this is true. He seems uneasy, so she picks up the bed sheet and wraps it around them. "I want to know the story behind each scar, so that next time, I understand you completely and not get afraid of your scars."

"My father used to beat me with the closest thing he could grab," he says quietly, feeling so exposed for the first time in years. "This long one is when he threw a chair at me," he says, pointing at a big, straight scar with a dark centre. His voice is filled with so much fear that it seems it's his turn to break down. Neha gasps and covers her mouth in terror as he traces the long, painful-looking scar with his trembling index finger.

"I shouldn't have brought this up," she says. "I am sorry that—"

He pulls her up and quietens her with a kiss. "Don't be sorry. I want you to know everything about me, Neha," his shaky voice betrays the look of composture he is attempting to secure on his face.

Neha stares at him and wishes that she could somehow help him seek freedom from his fears. "Promise me, you won't get up from the bed," she says with a small glint of mystery in her eyes.

"Okay," he breathes, dumb-founded by this sudden, unprecedented request.

She pulls the bed sheet completely over him, and then she ducks out of sight beneath the sheet.

"What are you up to?" there is an edge of anticipation and impatience in his tone.

Once her lips touch the scar near his waist, he knows what's going to happen. Her lips move from his waist to his chest as she kisses each scar slowly, owning them and making them a part of her own life.

"Neha!" His voice is rough, rich with desire.

Looking at him is as ecstatic as touching him. She can see his muscles flex as though she is actually touching him. His face creases with a grimace, his jaws clench.

Her hands have a will of their own, touching his back, his shoulders, sliding over the tough, hard flesh and relishing the strength beneath it.

"What's this one from?" Neha asks, tracing her finger along his back. It feels like it goes on perpetually.

"I accidentally broke my dad's Rum bottle," he manages to reply with quivering lips, remembering the incident. "It was standing at the corner of the dining table and I bumped into the table. My father beat me with the broken end of it."

"I'm sorry," Neha murmurs, touching the sore memory with her lips.

Tarun stretches into the burning caress and the haunting memories. It's like his brain is fighting over pain and pleasure. God, he doesn't know how much more he can bear.

She runs her hands further down his back. Eight… nine… ten… *God, how did he handle so much beating from his father, she wonders.*

"You're lucky to be alive, Tarun…"

"If I could, I would give away all my luck to Aditi."

"No!" Neha tells him calmly. "Don't think about it like that." She pushes herself up and presses her lips to his as she holds him close.

He looks so defeated, Neha almost starts apologizing, begging him not to be sad. But then, he straightens himself up and kisses her back.

"I want to start what we couldn't finish yesterday," she pleads.

"Okay, are you sure?" Tarun asks.

She nods silently and kisses him softly.

He opens his mouth, but pauses, "Okay. I get it, but just let me know at the first hint of uneasiness."

She pulls his arm gently and leans against him. He puts his arm around her shoulder and presses her close. "Work with me, sweetheart, so we can get rid of our past."

Neha reaches up and places her hands behind his neck. He leans down and puts his face in the crook of her neck, breathing her in. Her hair being pulled to one side is sexy as hell. She turns her head to look at him and gives him a radiant smile.

"Tarun," she murmurs.

In that moment, he feels the need to kiss her more than ever. He leans a little closer, closing the space between them. Hesitating, giving her the opportunity to stop him but she doesn't.

When his lips touch hers, he feels the tremor in his hands. She must have felt it too because she places her hands over his as he continues to caress her cheeks while he kisses her. She opens her mouth and he slips his tongue inside. The taste of her on his tongue causes him to release a deep moan. Neha slows down the kiss and rests her forehead against his chest.

"Tarun."

"Mmm." He is again at a loss for words. *I have never felt this kind of connection with any other human being in my life.*

She grabs his hand and lays it over her heart. "This connection that makes my heart race is uncharted waters for me. I wish I could hold onto it and never let go." She sighs, "But I need all of you, Tarun."

His fingers trail from her neck to her breasts. "You are making me go crazy, Neha." She presses her head deeper into the pillow as he circles her globes, a whimpering little moan leaving her lips.

Neha watches as she drags her eyes open, her hand going to his fingers to pull them down to where she needed him most.

His fingers edge beneath her panties and her hips arch closer to him. A gasp, then a hard breath of need parts her lips as he lets one finger slide into the narrow slit, feeling the slick wetness, the clench of her folds around his fingers.

Despite feeling so good, she is scared. She knows that any moment, she might spiral back to her nightmares.

"Stay with me, here, it's me Tarun," he murmurs in her ear.

As she hears his name and his voice, she snaps out of her thoughts and looks right into his eyes. She loves him and wants this more than anything else in the world.

Neha is breathing hard and fast beside him, little moans breaking past her lips. "I want you, Tarun."

He strokes her, rubs her, his finger thrusting lightly inside her. His thumb grinds against her and she feels her mind explode. Her senses disintegrate.

Right at this point, Dheeraj is going to come in. And ruin the moment. He is somewhere here, waiting for the right time to attack me.

"You are safe with me, Neha," Tarun says. "I am going to protect you."

Tarun's voice pulls her back into the feeling of pure love, far away from the darkness. Neha feels as though the world is burning around her, but for the first time, not with terror. It's pure pleasure.

His finger caresses her, thrusting inside just enough to stroke places she hadn't known she possessed. His fingers continue the search before finding a spot that sends her flying. Her hips arch, a cry throttles from her throat as he feels her core clench around his finger.

She was close. So close.

"You are safely tucked in your bed, with your love," Tarun says to ensure she doesn't spiral back. "I am giving you the pleasure you have always wanted and I love you."

She is gasping for breath. Short, startled cries leave her lips as he continues the rhythm, holding her close as shudders tear through her body.

Tarun pulls her back every time she is about to fall in to dark memories. A light flash suffuses her face and her soft pink lips part as she breathes in and out slowly. She closes her eyes as indescribable feelings rush up inside her, but all she sees is Tarun's smile and his stunning eyes.

Her orgasm is an explosion of sensation that tears through her, tightens her muscles and has her arching, crying, fighting to breathe.

"I liked that." A slow, blooming smile lights her face. "I loved that, Tarun," she says, as a happy tear makes its way from her eye to her nose.

"I am so happy for you, Neha. Happy for us." He bends, kisses the crown of her head and then pulls back slowly.

She tilts her head, staring back at him. "Thanks for being there, thanks for pulling me back to you."

But it was probably meant to be. And now that she has it, she wouldn't accept losing him. She wouldn't accept never taking a chance for him.

> "*We spend our lives planning a future. A future that may not exist.*
>
> *Then why not do whatever we can in the moment and enjoy every moment with our loved ones? Why wait for a difficult time to do this when time starts slipping away?*"

19

Last night had been a revelation for both of them. As they sat watching the sun set from Tarun's room, Tarun's phone buzzed for the hundredth time. He bent his head back and stared into the mobile screen, silently cursing his luck. "Oh god, how many times is she going to call me?"

"Is your mom calling you again?"

"Yes!" he answers as if muffling a scream.

Neha pauses the movie they have been watching and slides her arms around him. "Why don't you talk to her? She is all alone. She has lost her husband, and now a son," she says softly. "You should consider meeting her. It's not really her fault."

Tarun looks at Neha and vehemently shakes his head. "No!" What Neha has just said, remains in his head.

Tarun's mobile rings again, but this time, he answers the call. "Please listen to me," Tarun's mother says, in a pleading tone. "I am in Shimla, right outside your door. I need to see you for two minutes. Can you open the door?"

Tarun is frozen in the moment. He is not sure if he can face his mother. *How did she suddenly land up here?*

Tarun quickly rushes to his almirah and pulls out a fresh T-shirt, almost stumbling over as he runs towards the front door. "Please stay inside the room," he says. "I'll be back in no time." Then, as an afterthought, he adds, 'Can you maybe comb your hair and set the room straight a little, please? Just in case she comes in," he says as he eyes her top to bottom.

She hears the front door open up, "Tarun, are you here?" a deep female voice yells.

Neha combs her fingers through her tousled hair and walks to the bathroom door, but stops as she hears Tarun speaking in a loud tone. She doesn't mean to eavesdrop, but her curiosity gets to her.

"Mom, I don't want you to interfere," he says. "Please leave me alone." The pain in his voice is obvious.

Neha wants to run to him to hug him and comfort him.

"I know it's your life," his mom replies, "but it's her life too. Have you told her yet? Or no?" his mother says in a stern tone.

"I tried," he says, "but I can't!" He grits his teeth. "If I tell her, everything will get ruined. You don't understand, Mom!" Tarun says softly so that Neha doesn't hear him.

Neha is devastated by what he's just said. She doesn't want to pretend that she hasn't heard this and wants to go and ask him right away whatever he is hiding from her.

"The sooner you tell her, the less painful it will be. I don't want you to end up hurting her!"

"All my childhood went in pain because of my abusive father," he says and gulps down the pain. "And you did nothing about it. Now suddenly you want to show that you care?" Tarun yells. "Please go away and let me live the way I want to." He leaves the door open and stomps away to the living room.

Should I stay in here and pretend I didn't hear a thing? Should I walk into his room and confront him about whatever this secret is?

She steps outside the door and checks the alley. She doesn't want to confront Tarun's mother right now. But she wants to be with him. She walks up to him and sits beside him on the couch and hesitantly massages his back. He turns to her with sad, red eyes and winces before letting his shoulders relax. He doesn't want her to see him like this, he never does, but she has decided not to leave him. "Do you want to talk about it?"

He shakes his head in sad silence, without even looking at her. She sits as quietly, wrestling with the range of emotions going through her. She wants to be there for him, but she can't escape the sinking feeling in her stomach that whatever he's keeping from her could shatter her world into a million pieces. A voice inside her head is yelling for her to run before he has a chance to tell her.

Just then, the phone rings again. This time, it's Neha's. She stares at the screen.

Mom? Is the universe conspiring to spoil the best time of my life?

"Hello mom."

"Hello dear. How are you?" she asks warmly.

"I am okay, what about you?" Neha replies. She shows the phone screen with the word "Mom" displaying on the screen to Tarun.

"Well, we wanted to know about your holidays. Your dad needs to see if he can accommodate in between his official travel plans."

It's all your mistake. You never had the time for me. That's why this happened. You were so busy in your life that you didn't even bother to check my brother's holidays and sent me in advance to his place, to get rid of me. And yes, you did get rid of me. Emotionally!

"Well, I won't be able to come home," she says, blankly.

"Why?"

"I… I have extra classes," she says. "Also, I have been working as a lab assistant in the college for some learning and pocket money, just to keep myself busy."

"And what about the break when the semester ends?"

"Well, it's still far. I will check the college calendar and tell you," she says.

"Don't forget to do that."

"Sure," lies Neha. She has no plans of going back home. She wants to get the first possible job that can keep her away from the memories.

"You haven't called your brother for so long!" her mom says, and Neha feels butterflies in her stomach. "Why don't you call him?"

Now what can I tell her? That, whenever I talk to my brother, I remember the gory incident I do not want to remember.

"Oh, I am sorry. I have been occupied with college, assignments and then the lab assistant work," she says.

"Promise me, that you will talk to him?" her mother says sweetly, but she doesn't reply.

"Okay, I have to go," Neha replies abruptly. She wants this conversation to end.

"Bye dear, hope to see you soon," her mom says before disconnecting the call.

Maybe, deep down my heart, I know it's not really her fault. But, I don't want to go back to a life which keeps reminding me of what happened to me. I want to start afresh with someone I can trust. I guess, I have found that someone.

Neha keeps the phone on the bed and turns around to look at him. She pulls him towards her for a quick kiss on his lips and then, lies back down close to him.

She snuggles up on his lap and her eyes fall on the wall clock. "You haven't actually eaten anything since morning. I will go grab something for you and then, you need to take your medicines."

"Umm okay," he replies in a relaxed tone, as he realizes that Neha isn't going to push him into speaking about the incident with his mom.

She gets up swiftly and as she is about to get down from the bed, Tarun grabs her arm and pulls her back. He lowers his head and kisses her. Opening his lips, he deepens the kiss, drinking in her taste.

"Neha?"

"Yes?"

"It's great to feel loved and to have you by my side. No one has ever worried about me and you are worrying over every small thing that happens to me. You're the best girl that I could have ever found in the whole universe," he murmurs in her ear.

"You're straight out of fairy tales for me, Tarun. I have found you after really rough times. And I want to give all the world's happiness to you. Wouldn't you do the same if I needed you?"

"I would!" he says confidently.

"I would too." It was like a vow they made. A vow they meant to keep.

The first day of the semester break is a beautiful day, and Neha decides to spend it with Tarun. Even Ritu is out, probably with Gaurav. On a usual holiday, Neha would just lie down and read a book, but today is different. She has Tarun in her life and she wants to spend all the time with him.

The sun is shining bright in the sky, forcing away the winters. A welcome change from the cold days.

"I think it is going to be the best day of my life," chirps Neha as she walks towards Tarun's apartment. She briskly walks to where he lives and rings the bell gently. But no one answers. Wondering, she presses the bell two-three times and waits for a response. Nothing.

For some strange reason, she feels worried and wants to get inside the apartment. She looks around to make sure no one's watching and then tries the door handle. To her surprise, the door is open. She wonders why it isn't locked, but steps inside to check on Tarun.

The stillness of the living room is strange.

"Are you there, Tarun?" Neha shouts as she steps towards his bedroom, her anxiety increasing with each step. Closer to his room, she hears water running in the bathroom, so she slowly knocks on the bathroom door, hoping that Tarun would answer. But again, she receives no response.

She slowly pushes down the door handle and opens the door. The water is flowing down at full throttle from the tap and Tarun is bent over the wash basin with his elbows placed on it for support.

She takes two-three tentative steps towards him and places her palm on his back to give him comfort. "I am here for you, Tarun. It'll be okay."

With her warm words, he pulls over the hand towel and starts to wipe his lips and the tears from his eyes. Neha holds him close and takes the hand towel, helping him to clean up properly.

"How did you get inside?" he finally says with a ragged breath.

"I rang the bell, but there wasn't any response. When I tried the door, it was open, so I came in. What's happening, Tarun?" Neha asks, as she moves her fingers to comb his hair back.

"My mother must have gone to the market to get something. She must have left the door open, as she isn't familiar with the lock mechanism."

"Oh okay," she replies, not knowing what to say.

"And where's Gaurav? I haven't seen him either?"

"This is not how I want you to see me. Please go back to college and we can meet when I am a little better."

Neha does not listen to him. "Since, when have you been like this?"

"Can't say, maybe an hour or more. I think I have some viral infection or something like that," he replies, placing his hand over his forehead.

"I want to be here and make sure you're okay, Tarun," she says firmly.

"I don't think that is a good idea. I don't want you to get sick too," he tries to give a hollow logic.

"I am not listening to any of that crap. You need me and I will be here." She moves closer to him and moves his chin up with her fingers.

"Okay! Let me just clean up and look handsome again. Then, you can put me to sleep. I think some rest will help me recover from it." He tries to smile. He looks in a really bad shape – his skin is white and loose, his eyes are red and his forehead and hair are wet with sweat.

"You need some help with the shower," she says.

"Well, that's an offer I would never deny, but right now, I just want to take a quick one and come out." He winks at her, trying to mask the pain his eyes reflect.

"Fine! Just don't lock the bathroom door," she says, running her palm along his jawline.

Neha moves back to the bedroom and paces to and fro. She hears the bathroom door open and Tarun walks out in a white Polo t-shirt and track pants. He has combed his hair backwards and is looking cleaner, though his sickness is still pretty evident.

"Come, I will put you to sleep," she says, with a smile.

"That sounds like a splendid idea," he says. He kisses her on her forehead. "Thanks for being there."

"I am sure you would have done the same for me."

"I would do anything for you Neha," he says and kisses her on her cheek.

> *"When someone you love so deeply is battling an illness, all you can do is be present and show love in any way possible. Instead of being frustrated about what you cannot control, find small ways to love and be present every day, like making each other laugh, sharing words of affirmation, and simply holding each other's hands."*

20

It's been a full day but Neha hasn't heard from Tarun. She messages him a couple of times but receives no response. She can feel that something is seriously wrong and this feeling is making her heart sink.

The moment her classes finish, Neha takes out her mobile and calls Tarun. The phone keeps ringing for a long time until a female voice answers it. "Hello?"

"Er…" Neha moves the phone from her ear and checks the screen again to make sure she dialled the correct number.

"Hi! I wanted to check if Tarun is feeling better?" she stammers.

The line goes silent for a few seconds. Finally, she hears Tarun's mother breathe heavily into the phone. "Tarun is hospitalized."

Neha is unable to breathe. She chokes on the cold air and manages to say, "What?"

"He didn't want me to tell any of his friends about how he is."

"I am coming there. It doesn't matter what he thinks."

"It's totally your wish," she says. "But come with a strong heart. What you might hear may not be good."

What the hell is she talking about! What's wrong with Tarun? Why hasn't he told me anything?

Neha tightens her grip on the phone, notes down the address of the hospital with her trembling hands and disconnects after a feeble, "I am coming."

The moment Neha enters the hospital, the distinctive sterile smell floods her senses. She calls Tarun's mother and asks her the room number. "He is in room 212 on the second floor."

She runs up the stairs and reaches room 212 and looks inside from the small glass on the wooden door. She sees Tarun's mom standing next to her son, who is lying down and looking in the other direction. He looks really pale and weak.

Neha feels like running and taking him into her arms. Maybe that can make some of his pain go away.

She slowly opens the door and peeps in to make sure she isn't disturbing any family conversation.

"Tarun, you need to tell her, *now*! Or I am going to," his mom says affirmatively.

Tarun suddenly realizes that Neha is at the door and looks at her.

"I am sorry I didn't mean to interfere, but I got really worried."

"That's alright," his mother responds. "I have been looking forward to meet you, but didn't know that our first meeting will be at a hospital." She smiles sweetly at Neha.

His mother looks at Tarun, "She is even more beautiful than what you had described."

"Mom," he says.

His mother turns towards Neha. "I am sorry we have to meet like this, but I am happy that he has you."

"I am really happy to see you too," Neha replies softly.

"It's good that you are here. I need to go and manage some things at home. Would you mind staying over?" She says as she turns back to look at Tarun. "Also, Tarun needs some private time with you. He wants to talk about something."

She turns around and pats Neha's head lightly, as if giving her a blessing before she leaves the room.

Neha walks closer to Tarun and holds his hand. "What happened Tarun? How are you feeling?"

Tarun does not respond. It's as if he has an internal conflict going on between his heart and brain. As if he is pondering whether he should tell Neha everything or not.

He sums up his courage and finds some words. "Neha, you know you mean the world to me."

Neha's eyes get filled up with tears as she hears his shaky voice. She tries to nod as she holds back her tears. "I am scared, Tarun. What is wrong with you?" Neha asks, as she bursts into tears. Tarun is unable to see her cry and he turns and faces the window.

"Please tell me what's going on?" she pleads him, wiping away the tears that managed to escape her eyes.

"I can't—".

She slowly walks and stands to the side he is facing. She kneels down so that her face is at the same level as his. "Whatever it is, Tarun, please tell me." She wraps her hands around his.

Tarun tries to shake her hand off, but she doesn't let him go. He tries to stop the tears which are pooling in his eyes. He seems to be in a lot of pain, but he is still acting strong.

"I have been so submerged in my own pool of problems that I never saw your problems coming in," she says. "Please tell me what's going on. I beg you, Tarun."

"I am suffering from…"

"What is it? You can tell me." She holds his cheeks in her palms to comfort him.

"I have *cancer*!" he finally says with anger in his tone.

She has never seen him so angry. What she just heard makes her wonder if all this is a nightmare.

This can't be happening. Not to him. Not to us. Not now. "This can't be true."

As she looks at him, she sees tears slipping away from his eyes despite his control. She cannot see him like this.

"Please say that this isn't true."

He shakes his head in despair. "It's true, Neha. I have cancer."

Neha feels a chill run down her spine as her emotions go beyond her control and she sobs loudly.

"No! This cannot happen, you cannot—" she falls short of words as her sadness creates a vacuum in her throat.

"Neha, I don't want you to cry. I can't see you like this. I didn't mean to hurt you," he reaches out for Neha's hand. "I should have told you earlier."

Neha falls on the floor, falling short of air. She can't manage the pain. She can't believe this is happening to him.

What can you say to someone who has told you that he has cancer? What words can reduce the pain of a person suffering from a nearly fatal disease? What words can tell him that it's going to be alright? What words can console him into believing that the time that is waiting for him is not going to be tough?

She tries to stand next to the hospital bed again, and tries to brush his cheeks with her trembling hands. He looks right into her eyes, rather than looking away.

"There is a way we can correct this, right? I am sure there is a cure?"

He gulps in some air and says, "They are trying chemotherapy, which is making me feel more sick."

"But isn't that supposed to cure you?"

"The chances are very bleak."

"What kind of cancer? Is it bad? Since when do you know?" Neha asks, tears welling up in her eyes.

Tarun tells her what he knows and then adds, "I don't know exactly how bad it is, but it sure doesn't sound like a ride in the park."

Neha is devastated. She looks at Tarun with desperation in her eyes. "What happens now?"

"My mother is going to come and stay with me. I started chemotherapy a few weeks back. It all depends if my body's immunity works to fight this disease." Tarun pulled his shoulders to his ears. "That's all I know so far. And I'd really appreciate it if you could just behave as normal as possible around me. Also, nobody else needs to know about it. I don't want anyone's pity."

How did we get here? We can't be so unlucky. We had a difficult childhood, a difficult college life filled with nightmares and now, when everything seemed to be going in the perfect way, this happened.

"You don't lose hope. We are meant to be together. But for now, we have no other choice, but to follow the doctors' protocol and fight cancer, together," replies Tarun.

The doctors were not sure, but Tarun was hopeful and thought that he could beat this cancer. He was still young, and other than that, in good shape. He wasn't a smoker or drug addict, which would surely be an advantage now. He had seen the worst time in his childhood and now, when he had found the love of his life, he wanted to fight any obstacle to be with her, forever.

She rubbed Tarun's back. "I will take care of you. I will be your strength, just like you have been mine," Neha says, assuringly.

Tarun tries to steady his breathing, pressing his lips together. The bad thing was that his body was revolting against the poisonous chemo cocktail and not the cancer.

"If I could, I'd throw up for you, you know that," Neha says.

He smiled at her sweet comment and took her hand.

Neha is by Tarun's side most of the time. He doesn't know how she manages his grumpy behaviour and still be cheerful to bring him something good to eat, read or find a new series to watch on Netflix.

At first, the chemotherapy was bearable for Tarun. He slept a lot and all the tests, shots and other treatments he had to endure, he just let it pass by. He didn't think too much about the future. He wanted to believe the doctors, but he didn't want to undermine fate.

Gaurav was a good support in all this. They passed the time, playing video games or just sitting together and playing poker with Ritu and Neha.

Whenever he was by himself in the hospital room, he felt utterly lonely. If he needed fresh air, he would just walk slowly with the nurse to the window as he didn't have much energy left in him. Since the chemo medicine killed both the good and the bad cells in his body, it was a struggle to even do mundane things.

In the next two weeks, Tarun loses most of his hair and was afraid how Neha would react to his appearance.

Neha attends college regularly, but continues to think about Tarun. She calls him during the break to make sure he isn't feeling alone.

"Hi Tarun, I miss you so much," she says as soon as he picks up.

"I miss you too. It's very lonely here without you. I thought about taking up knitting today. Maybe, by the time I get cured, I would have knitted a really nice sweater for you."

She laughs at his joke to keep his spirits high. She is supportive and doesn't let him feel that she pities him. "How are you?" she asks.

"I have been better. I lost all my hair and the dark circles under my eyes reach down to the floor. Just wanted to let you know that you don't mistake me for our bald mathematics teacher the next time you see me.'

"Ha ha. Ya right! I can recognize you with my eyes closed, Tarun. I can feel you, breathe you." She sighs. "I guess, we all knew this would be a side effect of chemo. Anyway, I will come by in the evening after college. I hope you can give me some time," she continues to joke.

"Let me check my busy calendar. I can fit you in between watching *Two and a half men* in the morning and flirting with the nice nurse, who is older than my mom."

"Great, then it's a date!" she says.

At 3.30 p.m., someone knocks at Tarun's door. He knows it is Neha, by the careful manner in which the door is opened. It gives him enough time to place his phone back on the bedside table. He had been flipping through their pictures, wondering if they would ever have the great times again.

"Your new haircut suits you. You could still join the army with that," were her first words.

"Unfortunately, that's not my priority."

"So, how have you been?" she asks Tarun.

"Actually, I didn't know it was possible to feel so crappy. Everything hurts, everything upsets my stomach. I wish I could exchange my body for another one." Tarun stares at the wall.

"I don't know how I would endure it." She sighs.

"I'm glad you are here, though." Tarun smiles at her.

"Well, I took permission from your mother and the doctor," she says.

"Permission? For what?" Tarun cannot understand what she is saying.

"Well, I have taken their permission to take you out for a day."

"Well, I have got pretty bored looking at these grey hospital walls and wearing this apron like cloth, which hardly covers my body," Tarun says.

Neha giggles. Even in so much pain, he is trying to keep his spirits high. This is what she loves about him. He's given her the strength to face her fears and even now, he is fighting against his own.

"Here, you can wear these! She hands him a bag of clothes that she has got from his home.

Tarun looks at her and smiles. She helps Tarun change. Though, he has gone weak, the very fact that he is going out of the hospital has given him some extra energy.

"So, are we going to Switzerland?" he jokes.

"Would be cool, but I thought about something around here. Wait till I take you to the Shimla lake. It will be more beautiful than Switzerland."

"Really?"

"Yes, because you will be with me."

21

They arrive at the lake shortly and have lunch in the garden beside it. Though it is packed lunch, it feels special sitting and eating it there, under the open sky in each other's company.

She has planned everything for him, a nice floral bed sheet, picnic basket, healthy food, water and even some back-up medicines.

"I can't believe I am out of that godforsaken hospital. Everything seems so nice here."

Neha laughs. "I love your excitement. Just like a child's."

"I'm just happy to be under the open sky," Tarun replies.

After lunch, they walk to the lake. The trees are lined up on the waterfront and green branches are hanging into the water. In the middle of this idyllic scene was a little cottage, which is like a garage for small boats.

There is an entrance with a dusty counter on the far side of the water. As they wait there, they hear footsteps and shortly afterward, an old man arrives. He is dressed in jeans and a check shirt and from his sweat, they can guess that he must have been working.

They pay for two hours and the man takes them inside the cottage where all the boats are stored. He hands them some life jackets. The centre of the cottage is hollow and open so that the water can float inside. Some boats are already in the water; others pile up along the walls.

Neha climbs on to the boat and steadies it for Tarun. Once they sit down, the old man gives them a little push into the water and so they are under the evening sun and over the beautiful lake.

"It's beautiful," Tarun leans back.

"Look, how nice it is with the trees surrounding the water and the blue sky in the background."

He wants to paddle the boat, but she doesn't let him exert at all. With a few paddles, she moves them further out on the lake.

Tarun looks around, and for the first time, he feels tiny on that big lake.

"Why is life giving me so many challenges?" says Tarun.

"Tarun," she takes his hands into hers. "I didn't believe it myself when you told me. But, what we need to do is be more positive. We need to just live in the moment and feel that there's nothing better than sitting in the boat under the open sky."

Tarun smiles. She is right. He is having a really good time.

They sit there for a few more minutes, cuddled together, looking at the sky, just soaking in the nature and the positivity that this place emanated.

"Are you asleep?" she asks after a while.

"No, only daydreaming and enjoying the moment," Tarun responds without opening his eyes.

"We probably have to head back soon, before the sun sets."

"I know. But I'm so comfortable here." He takes in a deep breath.

They lie down in the boat together, holding each other so close, never to let go.

When they reached the cottage a while later, she rows directly into the opening and the old man is there to help secure the boat.

"Did you have a good time?" she asks Tarun politely.

"Yes, this was perfect, thank you!" Tarun responds. "I truly love you and spending time with you is a lot of fun." He nudges her before saying, "You're such a great girl. I am so lucky to have you."

"So, doesn't this great girl deserve a great kiss?"

Before she can finish her sentence, Tarun cups her face and pulls her closer.

He presses his lips to Neha's and kisses her with so much passion that she can feel his love and his pain at the same time. Neha wraps her arms around him and covers his lips in soft kisses, telling him that he is the love of her life.

"I love you, forever," she says.

"I love you too," he says, "for all my life and beyond."

Back at the hospital, Neha stays back with him. She checks if they have everything they need for the night and then, wishes Tarun good night. Unlike Gaurav, Ritu or Tarun's mom, she does not sleep on the couch. Instead, she makes space on the hospital bed and lies down next to Tarun. Holding him close, wanting to never let him go.

"Would you be able to sleep on this small bed?" Tarun asks.

"Shouldn't be a problem. I'm so tired, it's a mystery how I didn't fall asleep in the boat itself." She smiles and takes away all his uneasiness. "Besides, I feel more cozy and warm next to you."

She snuggles closer to him. "Thank you for everything, Neha." He puts an arm around her small figure and hopes that it isn't too much weight on her.

"I love you," Neha whispers.

"Forever," he says, as he kisses her forehead.

> "*It is in difficult times that you realize who your true friends are and what they mean to you.*"

22

"Not so well," Tarun hears his mom say in a hushed voice. She is talking on the phone in another corner of the hospital room, thinking he is asleep.

"He should have entered remission by now. That's when his body should have stopped producing cancer cells." There is silence. Tarun imagines his mom hunched over the small table in the corner, holding her tired face with her free hand. He knows she is worried about him.

So is he! He opens his eyes and boxes into the wall, quickly thereafter regretting it because his hand throbs with pain. His inter-veins fluid line falls on him because he has ripped on it too much. His mom rushes toward him.

"Are you okay?" She is still holding the phone in her hand.

"Yes," Tarun says through gritted teeth, trying to shake the pain off.

"I'll call you back," Tarun's mom says into the phone. Then, she moves her chair closer to him and sits down.

"I don't want you to feel disappointed because the remission didn't show up in the report," Tarun breaks the silence.

"But—" She has lost all words.

"Don't be sad, mom. These are just procedures. Just because the doctor said remission should have started doesn't mean it's a problem if it hasn't. Our body is very complex and everyone's body may react differently to the medicine. Maybe I'll take some more time. But, I will get out of it," he says positively.

"I hate this cancer. I wish it would have never happened to you," she replies.

"I hate this cancer too. I should be enjoying first experiences of love and life instead of having an IV line of morphine in my arm, which by the way, makes it impossible to lie in any other position than that of an Egyptian mummy. I should be working extra hours after college, to save some money for travelling. I should be doing so many things, other than lying in this stupid hospital bed. And, that gives me even more strength to fight cancer."

"I cannot agree more."

"Ma, I will not let cancer win. But, I want to take a break from this chemo, so that my body can heal and fight back."

Tarun's mom nods with an earnest face, though her voice is soaked in concern. "But chances of the cancer cells revolting again will be higher that way."

"I know that, but if I keep staying in this hospital, I am sure I won't get cured. This isn't a life anybody wants to endure," Tarun says with a raspy voice.

"I will talk to the doctors and see if that is possible. Let's take the doctor's suggestion, and once you feel stronger, we can start the chemo again." She kisses his forehead, lovingly caressing the stubble on his head.

The doctors agree for a chemo break and Tarun gets up to go home.

Neha has been running around, making enquiries about a naturo-therapy doctor in McLeod Ganj. He is a ninety-year-old Tibetan doctor named Dr Yeshi Dhonden, quite well-renowned.

Neha travels to McLeod Ganj all by herself, in a public bus, stands in queues and gets medicines for Tarun. He knows how difficult it must have been for Neha to travel alone. Despite her fear of public places and crowds, she still went ahead. All she wants is for Tarun to be fine.

She has researched a lot about this Tibetan doctor and spoken to other cancer survivors online on Facebook. Tarun believes that he has more time left in his life with Neha. Together, they are all geared up to fight that disease.

Two months into his chemo break, along with having natural medicines and light, non-acidic food shows Tarun the first positive effects. He has more energy and can go for walks with Neha. He can get better sleep. To increase his immunity, Ritu makes him fresh pulp of Indian gooseberries and wheat grass, which he drinks every morning.

He is feeling better and his mom invites Neha, Gaurav and Ritu home for dinner. While the others enjoy the feast, Tarun enjoys the presence of his close friends and family along with the food.

"Well, you seem to have gotten stronger since you left the hospital," Gaurav says, looking at Tarun's empty plate. "Do you want more?"

"I'm good, thanks." Tarun smiles. "I had almost forgotten how good it was to actually enjoy food and good company."

"We are here for you," Gaurav says.

"We appreciate that." Tarun's mom smiles gratefully.

While Tarun had started the natural medicines against the doctor's advice, he couldn't deny that it was important to check the status of the disease and take corrective action.

After six months of natural medicines, he went for a check-up to see if there was any improvement in his health.

"How do you feel today?" The doctor asks him.

"Six!" he says, giving his comfort level a score out of ten.

"In the last few months, I have never heard you saying anything better than a four. This is better, but not perfect. We are getting there. At least your blood report shows improvement."

Tarun nods, pressing his lips together. "But you can't guarantee whether I can spend Diwali at home?" He really wishes for that to be possible, for his mother.

"Well, once we take your pet scan, the results of the same will be out in the next two or three days. Blood indicators are not conclusive. The pet scan will help us decide the next steps for your treatment."

Three days later, Tarun and his mom are called into the doctor's office at the hospital once more. His mom is really nervous and scared, but puts up a brave face for Tarun.

As they wait in the waiting room, he can hear the hands of the wall clock ticking. It seems as if a time bomb is ticking and he doesn't know when it would explode.

As the attendant announces his name, they walk in, only to realize the presence of four doctors inside the cabin, instead of the usual one.

"So, Tarun! I have good news for you. Not just one, but two," the doctor says and continues without a break. "Firstly, you can spend Diwali at home, and secondly, you finally entered remission. It is a miracle and all the doctors in our department have specifically double-checked your reports before we could give you this good news."

"Oh, that's wonderful!" Tarun's mom clasps her hands to pray.

Tarun releases a long breath. "That's a good start." He smiles.

"Yes, you are right! It's a start. Your next steps are to begin with radiation to make sure that no cancer is hiding in your body. Next, you will have daily oral chemo through tablets which you can take at home and once monthly at the hospital. Now, I'm pretty confident that you will be able to fight this cancer."

"Thanks," Tarun replies gratefully.

"I advise you to go home now and enjoy Diwali. Celebrate this first achievement and live every day."

Tarun nods. "Thank you." He shakes hands with all the doctors and leaves for home.

In the hallway, his mother pulls him into a surprise hug and squeezes him until he doesn't have any air left. She has tears streaming down her face. But this time, they are tears of happiness.

"Mom, you're choking me!" He breathes.

She holds on to him a little longer and kisses his forehead. "I'm so happy." She lets him go and wipes her tears. Then, she squeezes his shoulders. "The important thing is that you made it to the next stage. Even though it's going to be hard, at least we know it's working and the natural treatment is making you better. You have to thank Neha for finding you those medicines."

Tarun picks up his mobile and calls Neha to give her the slightly good news.

"Oh, I am so happy for you." She literally jumps up with joy. "I knew it, I knew it!"

"Thanks Neha. I couldn't have done it without you."

"Oh! You don't have to thank me. If I start thanking you, then the list is going to be really long." Tarun just smiles. "But yes, you owe me because I had to travel in a bus, full of strangers."

"I owe you everything, Neha."

"And I owe my life to you, Tarun. I love you so much."

On Diwali, his mom and Gaurav decorate the whole apartment with lights. Tarun looks at Gaurav and wonders where he's got all the energy from. In the last so many years, Gaurav has never decorated the apartment for Diwali. *Maybe they all want to make him feel livelier and happier.*

During the day, Tarun is surprised to have received so many WhatsApp messages. So many people wish that he gets better quickly. It touches him to see how they all care about him, even those people whom he hardly knew in college.

But he feels tired from all the excitement. He goes to lie down for a while. He must have slept for several hours because it is already dark in his room when he opens his eyes again. He can make out a shape next to his bed. After rubbing the last bit of sleep out of his eyes, he tries to put a face to this shape. Many times in the hospital, he had fantasized about Neha, sitting by his hospital bed. Therefore, he turns his head to the ceiling to clear his thoughts and then, closes his eyes again. The next time he would open them, she would be gone. It has happened many times.

Except that this time, someone touches his hand. He keeps his eyes closed and enjoys the sensation of Neha's soft hands, which he recognizes so well. Her eyes gleam in the dark, a crooked smile trying to hide how overwhelmed she is. He sits up and she lets go of his hand.

Her expression becomes serious. "So, how are you now?"

"Better! I'm more positive. I have some hope about actually surviving." He longs to hold her hand again and moves a little closer to the edge of the bed, hugging her.

"I'm glad to hear that." She closes her eyes and takes a deep breath in his embrace.

"I have slept long enough. Let's go down! Are Gaurav and Ritu here?" Tarun gets out of bed.

"Yes, they are in the living room. They wanted to give us some privacy."

They head down to the living room and he is greeted by his cheerful friends. He can feel the concern and warmth in their hugs.

There was a delicious home-cooked meal comprising of *poori aloo* and *kheer,* his favourite dishes that his mother used to cook for him every Diwali. They all munch the food while Tarun eats very less. He isn't allowed fried food, not yet. He has his bowl of healthy food that tastes bland, but just looking at the good food around and happy friends enjoying it, he feels great. Afterwards, they play *teen patti* – the Indian version of poker, which has been a tradition associated with Diwali night – until well after midnight.

That night makes him feel that there is a lot of life left in him. He wants to fight this disease completely out of his body.

They hug their goodbyes. It is the happiest night Tarun can remember in a long time. He wants it to last longer. Maybe, forever.

Tarun isn't sure about forever, but he knows too well that today his mind is at ease, and his heart full of hope.

He is sure that he belongs to Neha and he has to fight this disease to make sure he can be with her forever.

> "*Forever is such a powerful word and yet we take it for granted.*"

23

Tarun continues the natural medicines, simple vegan food and then, starts with radiation in the next month. It is a painful process and it dries out his skin. It is so unhealthy for people that he is the only one allowed in the room when the laser is on. While he is by himself in that room, the doctors or nurses monitor him and talk to him via a microphone and speakers. The voices sound hollow and slightly bizarre. He has made a game out of it, pretending that it is god talking to him.

"Tarun, how are you feeling?" God is female today.

"You know, god, it could actually be better. I'd like to file a few complaints."

God ignores him.

"Just tell us in case you feel more pain than normal or if you get dizzy."

"You haven't answered my question from last time. If I die, can I jump from one cloud to the other and would I fall back down to earth if I missed. Or can I fly anyway?"

There is silence. God always takes his sweet time to answer.

"I'd like to keep you on earth for a while. You'll only need to know this if you actually get there."

"Can you see in the crystal ball and confirm that I will live?" God keeps silent.

"Can you at least tell me how long I have to bear this pain?"

"Fifteen more minutes." God likes to stay mysterious.

Once Tarun is dressed and back on his bed, the nurse brings him some water. "There's no water in heaven, so have as much as you want on earth. In heaven, you just get to drink wine." She winks at Tarun.

It's fun as she continues to pretend to be god and keeps his spirits up. Tarun smiles and sips the water. It feels good.

Another six months have passed. Tarun and his mother are called into the doctor's office again. The expression on his face is serious, but his eyes have a mysterious sparkle about them.

"So, Tarun, your latest scans are thoroughly checked and I'm very happy to announce that you are cancer free." The corners of his mouth turn slightly upward.

Tarun and his mom exchange a glance, as if to get reassurance that they had heard the same thing.

"This is amazing news!" His mom's face lights up and she jumps up from her chair to hug Tarun.

"Yes." Tarun laughs whole-heartedly, after what seems like a lifetime.

The doctor nods. When they are all seated again, he continues. "This means," he looks at Tarun, "that there will be no more aggressive treatment now. You just have to give your body a well-deserved rest and then get it back on track. Which means, take necessary vitamins and don't overstrain yourself with physical work."

"Okay," Tarun says.

"Your bones are fragile at the moment and your heart and liver have worked overtime," he explains. "We will have some check-up appointments throughout the next few months to make sure that no cancer has returned. But other than that, you can slowly return to a normal life now.'

"Normal life! That sounds magical," Tarun says excitedly.

"How likely is it that the cancer would return?" Tarun's mom holds her breath at the pertinent question.

"I don't want to give you a percentage here, but with Tarun's age and health, I'm quite positive that it won't return. Though we can never be hundred percent sure."

"Focus on your achievement for now. In six months, you come back for the next pet scan. Until then, there is no need to worry unnecessarily."

Tarun was speechless. His mother asks the questions for him. "He doesn't need to come back to the hospital for six months?"

"Yes, and then in another half a year."

"Wow!" Tarun says, still absorbing the happy shock.

"I'm so grateful," Tarun's mom says when they walk towards the car. "What should we do to celebrate? Dinner at a fancy restaurant?"

"I still can't believe this! When we leave now, does it really mean I'm not coming back this week?"

"Yes!" His mom beams.

"This will be almost weird," Tarun laughs.

When he is alone in his room later that day, he looks at himself in the mirror. For the first time in a long time, he can look at his body without staring in disgust, unsure of where the enemy was hiding. Now, he just wonders whether he'd feel it if the cancer returned. Would he notice it early enough this time, that at least it would never get that bad again?

The next thing he wants to do is inform Neha. But, in a special way.

He texts her. *I will be coming to your apartment in the evening.*

Sure, I will finish classes and come early, but Ritu is home. She will let you in if you reach early.

His phone beeps again. *Any update from the doctor?*

Not yet. He doesn't want to break the news on a phone call. He wishes to surprise her and see her reaction.

Tarun plans a great evening with Neha. He plans to cook for her. Ritu and Gaurav help buy the ingredients for him. He reaches her place and Ritu shows him where everything is kept in the kitchen.

Gaurav hugs him tight. "Bro, I am so happy for you. I knew you were a fighter."

Tarun hugs him back tightly. "I couldn't have done this without you guys. I lost hope every day, but then I got back hope when you all stood by me." Ritu is standing a bit away, with tears in her eyes. She comes running upon hearing this, and hugs both of them.

"Hey, you are crushing me!" Tarun says, and they all start laughing with tears rolling down their eyes.

They leave after some time, giving Tarun and Neha the personal space they need. Neha arrives from college and he opens the door for her.

She hugs him and asks. "So what's the plan?"

"I'm going to cook for you."

"You can cook?"

"Don't sound so surprised. I am not that bad. Tonight, I'll give you the taste of a fine dining restaurant at home. Come!"

"And what's on the menu?"

"We're having biryani, potatoes and raita. All cooked specially by your personal chef, Tarun." He bows and she comes forward to kiss him excitedly.

"Can I help you with something?" she asks him, while sitting at the table.

"Nope, everything is ready. All you need to do is eat. And then, finish off with your very own special dessert."

"Oh wow! We have dessert too? What would that be?"

"Me!" Tarun smiles, taking a bow.

"Aww, in that case, I want to have the dessert first." She bends and kisses Tarun again.

"The fruit of patience is sweet. So, you'll have to first have dinner."

"First, you tell me what the smile, that's glued to your face, is supposed to mean."

Tarun turns to her with a grin. "I wanted to wait until I'd be ready with something to toast, but since you asked," Tarun paused for a moment to raise the suspense, "I'm cancer free."

Her lips curl up in a smile, but her eyes tell a different story. The corners of her mouth quiver. She puts her hands in front of her face. "That's so good to hear," she breathes heavily. "I am so happy for you." There are tears in her eyes as she comes close to Tarun and hugs him.

On feeling the warmth of his body, she cries out heavily. "Oh, I thought I had lost you. I was so broken."

"Hey, everything is alright now. Stop crying!" He tries to wipe her tears with his thumb, but they keep pouring.

"It was so difficult to act strong in front of you. Please let me cry." And she continues to cry as he holds her in his arms.

They go for a walk along the hill and Tarun cannot stop staring at how her long hair flowed over her back, like a waterfall that glistered in the sunlight with every step they took.

He, on the other hand, has styled his hair in a crew cut and is wearing a cap most of the time. He usually put it on backward to appear a little cool.

They sit down on a bench facing the hills as the sun spreads a crimson color across the sky.

"You look a lot better every day," she says, after they have walked in silence for a while. "Being a strong and healthy man suits you."

"Thanks for the compliment, I guess. I couldn't have done it without you. You know that, dont you?" Tarun asks.

"And I love you more than my life, you know that, don't you?" she asks.

"I love you, Neha. Oh god, I love you so much."

Tarun looks out into the horizon. He starts drawing a mental picture of the home that he wants to with Neha.

"I've never been so happy in my life," Neha says, turning to look at Tarun.

Tarun matches her smile as he says, "I feel the same way, my love. I just wish we can have such evenings forever."

We will. "You are my love forever," Neha says.